INS Chanakya

Indo-China War, Volume 1

Pranjeet Sarkar and Aayushya Verma

Published by Aayushya Verma, 2021.

INS CHANAKYA

First edition. November 27, 2021.

Copyright © 2021 Pranjeet Sarkar and Aayushya Verma.

ISBN: 979-8223817130

Written by Pranjeet Sarkar and Aayushya Verma.

Table of Contents

The book is dedicated to all the soldiers who lost thier life while serving the nation.

INDO-CHINA WAR 2038

INS CHANAKYA

The warship that changed the war

PRANJEET SARKAR

AYUSHYA VERMA

INS Chanakya

[The Story of a Warship that turned the tides]

Written By: Pranjeet Sarkar

Co-Written By: Ayushya Verma

In the year 2038, tensions between India and China were constantly rising since over a decade due to their territorial and trade dispute. The Malacca disaster spiraled the tensions into an all out war. The Indians stroke first, attacking all Chinese military positions in Aksai Chin and seized all disputed territory overnight in a Blitzkrieg style strategy.

On May 26, twelve days after the Malacca disaster the two countries broke decades old peace treaties and officially declared war on each other. The initial misconception spread in the international media that any conflict between the two nations would end in a swift Chinese victory was shattered beyond repair.

It seemed that the forgone conclusion that the numerically superior Chinese forces would advance quickly into Indian Territory without any resistance, was wrong to the core as they met with stiff defense and resistance from not only the Indian forces but the citizens as well.

The numerical superiority of the Chinese was countered the highly trained and efficient Indians. The marching Chinese were often led into traps or the supply chain was destroyed, leading to quite hardships in the north. Though the Chinese managed to cut off North East via the Siliguri Corridor[1], they suffered quite losses when Pakistan jumped in and lost much of its territory. The new silk route was also affected as trade began to dry up in the area.

The global economy fell in shambles and as it plunged into recessions, efforts from the global community to enforce a peace treaty against two warring nations increased. With China cutting off the chicken's neck and capturing the entire north-eastern states of India along with Bhutan, Nepal and parts of West Bengal; India seized parts of Pakistan along with some parts of Tibet and Xinjiang.

Both countries were unwilling to accept either a ceasefire or come back to the pre-war status quo. The two sides even went to the extent of missile exchange falling short of going nuclear because of international obligations. The war now continued in a stalemate for twenty months, with no end in sight as the nations long crossed the point of no-return. It has now become a conflict that would change geography and geo-politics of South Asia.

Though it seemed impossible at first – but the two nations had been preparing for a confrontation for perhaps decades. Even after constantly fighting for twenty months, the trades were relatively good with the nations and reinforcements were abundant.

China following its 'String of Pearls' doctrine, surrounded India by building bases in Myanmar, Sri Lanka and Pakistan. The Pakistan trade route and the military base were actively attacked by India but to no avail. Despite intense combat, the route was not disrupted beyond a few days.

The Indians had built multiple naval and airbases in Vietnam, Japan and Korea to counter the String of Pearls. This gave them access to the heavily disputed South China Sea and allowed some extent of control on Malacca Strait.

The Indian Navy now had two HQs after Vishakhapatnam, the previous HQ was blockaded by Chinese warships with a clear threat that any military action from the Indians on the ships would lead to a missile attack on all cities in range – Vishakhapatnam, Hyderabad, Puri, Chennai and Amravati.

Apart from Chennai, all other cities were left unscratched by the missile volleys – perhaps to make any misadventure more costly. Vishakhapatnam Naval Base was evacuated with all officers now assigned to either the Eastern or Bengal flank headquartered in Andaman and Nicobar Islands or Western flank also known as Arabian flank headquartered at Porbandar, Gujarat.

Camorta, Andaman and Nicobar Islands

It was January 17, 2040. A moderately cold day in the lower latitudes, the main port had limited visibility due to the mist but operations were conducted properly. Before the war began, it was a civilian and cargo port but after the blockade of Vishakhapatnam – Camorta now acted as Indian Navy's main battle port for Eastern flank.

It was 6 in the morning and the shift at the port was changing when everyone heard an alarm. Sirens played in every loudspeaker on the island along with an announcement, 'THE PORT IS UNDER ATTACK. ALL CIVILIANS ARE REQUESTED TO EVACUATE TO NEARBY SHELTERS. VOLUNTEERS PLEASE HELP THE CIVILIANS FIND WAY. I REPEAT...'

Despite the initial panic, all civilians were moved away from the port to the shelters built underground in order to defend against missile attacks. The entire island was transferred to the shelters numbering a total of twenty. The volunteers tried their best to maintain calm among the civilians but they were not much effective.

People, in particular, the children were horrified by hearing the explosions from the surface. Parents tried their best to calm their wailing children, giving them hopes that everything will be okay. The bombardment on the surface continued for ten hours straight after which everything went silent.

Starting from the shelters in the port, the people began hearing footsteps outside their shelters. The volunteers continuously try to reach out to the higher ups for an update only to find complete radio silence. The door opened up with a 'BANG!!!' and about five soldiers entered the shelter.

Armed with assault rifles, one of the soldiers yelled something in an unknown language – leaving the people confused. A second one pointed to a device in his jacket's left pocket to which he smiled and pushed a button on it. He again spoke in a microphone and the voice in English emerged from a speaker near his shoulder. "This port is under Chinese control and all military personnel must surrender or else they'll be killed."

Before anyone could do anything, the group opened fire on the people killing all the people. Similar massacres happened all across the island with the Chinese soldiers killing even the civilians.

In a similar shelter underneath the single mall, everyone remained in a state of panic upon hearing the gunshots and explosions nearby except for a young lady in a casual shirt-trouser with heeled boots, who quietly observed the surroundings. She quietly got up and whispered to the volunteer, "The Island has fallen to the Chinese. We should move out fast or else we'll all be killed."

Initially shocked, the volunteer refrained from screaming and asked back, "Who are you? And how do you know whether the island has fallen or not." The lady bit her lip and responded, "I am on your side, that's what you should know for now, and now hurry up before the Chinese troops come here."

The volunteer didn't believe her words but agreed to evacuate the shelter after considering the fact that there is complete radio silence even after the fighting seemingly stopped. The bulky door was opened and all the occupants slowly came out and walked the corridors evading the prying eyes of security cameras.

The lady ordered the group to halt as she heard footsteps approach. Taking cover in an alley, she reached to her handbag to pull out a handgun. Equipping the silencer, she quietly waited for the person to approach. As the shadow of the mysterious person enlarged, she jumped in front of him/her and shot six times.

"Let's go!!!" She said calmly and made a gesture to the people to move. The group came out to see two persons in military uniform dead. They didn't seem Indian at all implying that whatever the lady said to the volunteer was truth. Stripping their weapons, the group continued to move on with two armed men with the lady at front and one with the volunteer looking for any pursuers.

As the group reached the main port, they hid in the covers of the containers spread across the port in disarray. "Come on, look. There's a cruise ship there." A woman from the group exclaimed and many people began running towards it only to be intercepted and attacked by the Chinese troops waiting for anyone to fall in their trap.

As some people begin to return after taking injuries, the group begins to run the other way with armed people firing at the pursuing Chinese. The lady led the group through a narrow bridge to another island and stopped in front of a bulkhead. She hit a panel at the side and the bulkhead began to open.

"Injured people first, then children and women. Armed men hold off the pursuers." She shouted and began shooting at the Chinese pursuers who in turn call for reinforcements. "Hurry up. Aah..." The lady suddenly takes a sniper hit in the arm and retreated behind a broken pillar. Her arm was bleeding and she applied pressure using her handkerchief before returning fire and killing the sniper atop the granary. "Is she a soldier?" Everyone gasps as they saw the near impossible deed but she gave no attention.

"Everyone's in." The volunteer shouted finally and the fighting force began to steadily retreat. The incoming soldiers began to gain on them and as everyone entered the bulkhead was sealed shut. "What now?" The citizens asked the volunteer who in turn looked towards the injured lady.

A man came up to her and gave her first aid. "Thank you." The lady said and he replied, "It's my job as a doctor. You're lucky the bullet didn't hit anything important but it'll be better if you'd refrain from using your right arm." The Chinese began to bang the steel bulkhead and cries could be heard ordering them to open the door and surrender.

"What are we going to do now? I hope you have anything that could lead us out of here or..." The volunteer asked the lady and she got up. Moving inwards she opened another bulkhead. All the lights present inside sprang to life and the people saw a ship.

It wasn't any ship though, it was a warship. The lady turned towards the crowd and began, "This is the latest ship of the Indian Navy – INS Chanakya. My name is Captain Amaira Gupta and I am the captain of the Chanakya." The crowd gasped in awe.

"Captain, we're really glad to see you back." A voice came from behind Amaira. She turned back to see three people in full naval uniforms emerge from the shadows and salute her. "Commander Naina, Lieutenant Arman and Lieutenant Vivaan I am really glad that you and the technical staff are here."

Naina came forward, "We're really sorry Captain but..." She couldn't finish as five people pulled out guns and shouted, "Freeze!!! We're taking you and that ship as hostages." Amaira reached out for her gun only to find it missing.

The emerged crew pulled out their guns but the traitors pointed their guns towards the other people, "Don't try anything smart or else, you'll be responsible if anything bad happens to these poor people." They gritted their teeth as they engaged safeties of their weapons and holstered them.

"Why are you doing this?" Amaira tried to negotiate and the man who seemed in-charge howled, "We were never on Indian side. We were sent here to work in order to monitor and report the activities of the Indian Navy. We were the ones who sent the reports about the numbers of defending ships and the ships that were supposed to dock."

The conversation continued as the other spies frisked the civilians and took away the weapons of the people who armed themselves. With all the civilians – men, women and children at gunpoint, the talking spy ordered Amaira "Open the bulkheads and let the Chinese soldiers enter. I promise, you'll be treated as POWs[2] and the civilians won't be harmed."

As he completed the sentence, a gunshot echoed in the chamber. A spy noticed a dent in the pipe next to him and pointed to a girl probably in the early teens holding a gun. "We made a mistake by not frisking the children. Now kid, quickly handover the gun if you don't want to get hurt." The girl obliged, activating the safety and put it on the floor before sliding it towards the spies.

The nearest spy picked up the gun and pointed his one at her, "You've missed li'l miss, but I won't." His finger squeezed the trigger when the girl smiled care freely. Everyone thought that she didn't know the gravity of the situation but...

The pipe hit by the bullet burst, spewing superheated steam on the assailants. They began to scream as the steam discharge burned their exposed body parts dropping their weapons. "I never aimed at you." The little girl said unsure whether they heard her. The next moment, the spies were hit by multiple bullets.

Amaira came to the girl and smiled, "Thanks kid. Would you tell me what's your name?" The girl spoke lightly, "My name is Ananya Anand." "You have my sincerest gratitude for all the actions. Now everyone here will board the ship."

2

In the bridge of Chanakya, there were only four navy officers present. "So, this is it? Only this much crew is left?" Amaira asked and Naina replied, "Yes. Other officers went out as well, just like you but they didn't make it back." "I don't even think they'll ever come back." The comment from Amaira shocked the trio.

"Why are you saying so?" Vivaan asked to which she replied, "I saw the bastards open fire and killing everyone in the shelters – soldiers or civilians. They didn't even bother to see if there were children." "But that's a total violation of all rules of war..." Amaira stopped Arman in his tracks, "There's only one rule in war victory washes away every dishonor. If we win, we can sue them for every war-crime as we please but so would they if they win."

"The ship was fully repaired just moments before the attack came but because of lack of crew and system faults, the higher ups didn't allow us to have it in battle." Naina gave a brief summary of the events that prelude the attack. "Well, it's good that we have this ship to escape from here. How's the stock? Do we have enough food and water for all those people?" Naina responded, "Yes, apparently we have stored enough that'll last us two months with a crew of seven hundred."

Amaira took a look at all the systems in the bridge "How's the background check going on of our guests?" Naina walks to the internal comm. station, "Captain, the crew has verified all the passengers – nothing to cause worry." Amaira sighed in relief, "Good that means we're good to go."

"Wait good to go, with four crew members." Vivaan asked and Arman replied, "Hey, I don't think we can do anything else. Let's get to a safe place before those counterfeiters see this ship and make a Made in China version." The joke helped relieve the grim atmosphere as the ladies giggled.

"Okay then, Lt. Vivaan you take the CIC[3], Arman you have the Radars. Naina take position as the XO[4] and have propulsion in your arm. I'll have the power and put all defenses and weaponry on AI." Amaira ordered. Vivaan interrupts, "Sorry captain but should I put main CIC on AI as well?" "No, use the second CIC. It's fully automated."

"Begin system checks." Naina orders and everyone starts to work on their systems. "All defensive systems check. CIWS[5], Missile batteries and launchers all good." "Navigation systems check. Monitoring radars all good but unable to connect to GPS." "SONAR systems check. No noise nearby." "Weapon systems online, Turrets loaded with single rounds. Feeder mechanisms all green."

"CIC systems check. All data links active, CIC working properly." "All nuclear reactors active. Critical in T minus 180." "All external communication systems working normally. No feed from satellite though." "All ship based Radars active." "Internal communication feed online." Amaira announced in the intercom, "This is the captain of the Chanakya. The ship will leave in T minus 150, all crew members proceed to their designated places."

• • • •

IN THE LIVING QUARTERS of the ship, people began whispering about the announcement, "Whoa I never thought I would be in a warship." Someone exclaimed, while a child clung to her mother, "I am very scared mommy." In the midst of all this, Ananya quietly sat in a corner when another girl sat in front of her. "What happened?"

Before she could answer, the girl began her introduction, "My name is Divya, Divya Shah. Thanks for saving us back them." Ananya slowly muttered, "Never mind. I just saved myself." Divya was taken aback but smiled, "What happened, you can tell me." "No thanks, I'll pass." She said curling herself into a ball.

. . . .

IN THE BRIDGE, AMAIRA ordered all propellers at 10 percent output as soon as the four nuclear reactors went critical. The ship slowly moved out of the island and discarded its camouflage. "Turn the ship north and try contacting headquarters." Vivaan immediately turned on all radars and began sending SOS calls on all frequencies.

. . . .

IN THE CAPTURED CAMORTA control center, the Chinese began to take over the structure with top officials of the Navy as prisoners of war. The radar installations that were damaged during the siege were being rebuilt quickly in order to manage and control the ship routes around the island.

The admiral was sitting in a lone cell with the admiral of Indian Navy's Eastern Flank. "Want a cigar?" He asked to which the Indian admiral politely refused. "You see admiral Abhijeet; I must admit that your troops fared quite well even in the most distressing odds. You took out half my total ships even when we outnumbered you five ships to one. Impressive."

Admiral Abhijeet gave a blank smile, "I know you're bluffing. Give me all the condolences you want, it won't change the fact that you killed all my subordinates after the surrender, Admiral Wang." Wang hissed under his breath, "You're getting all wrong ideas. I'll admit that it was a mistake from our behalf and we're ready to give an unconditional apology to every soldier's family regarding this incident but you should understand that in war everything is fair."

A soldier suddenly rushed in and saluted Wang. "Admiral, I have something that you should know." Wang gave a look to Abhijeet and turned towards the soldier, "Go on." "But Admiral..." Wang dismissed the soldier's concerns and the trio went to the main control room.

As they entered the control room, the guards were taken aback by seeing the POW there and trained their guns at him. "At ease, men.

He's here to witness the effectiveness of our naval command structure." The guards lowered their weapons and an officer began. "Sir, about two hundred seconds ago; we had a radar contact with an unknown ship. The ship appeared suddenly here – about twenty two nautical miles North West at 18.97 deg, stayed on radar for seventy seconds all the while continuously signaling SOS before disappearing."

Wang looked at the radar screen and asked, "Was it stationary or mobile." The operator took out a notepad and read, "Mobile, with speed five knots moving or drifting northwards." "North..." "Is it one of ours?" "Don't know, we didn't get any match from the records." Wang thought about it and ordered, "Inform the ships, they are to form a search fleet and intercept that supposed ship. If it's a friendly one, look for any assistance they might need. If it's an Indian ship, capture it." Two interceptors, a heavy cruiser and a destroyer were assigned the task which began to stock up on ammunition and supplies.

● ● ● ●

ON BOARD THE BRIDGE of the Chanakya, Arman realized his mistake of turning on all radar transponders as Amaira reproached him for that. Knowing that she'll have an interception fleet at their tail, Amaira orders propulsion to maximum in order to outrun them.

The ship was ordered to go northwards in order to escape the Chinese ships that were stationed near the main port. Going full speed at 43 knots, the pursuers had no chance of catching up against the over agile ship with their relatively sluggish movement at 35 knots.

But things didn't go well on the Chanakya. After about one and half hour of speed-run, the transmission began showing problems and soon the propellers shut down. "Damage report!!!" Amaira shouted and Naina immediately asked on the internal communication.

"Captain, we have some issues with power transmission, the maintenance crew is trying to rectify the problem." Naina reported.

"How much time before we can move?" Amaira asked and the response came, "A couple of hours probably."

A '*WHATTT!!!*' echoed in the bridge and Amaira asked the crew to hurry up. "We are severely short-handed and isolation of the fault is taking too long." She retorted, "Get us mobile ASAP." The maintenance head sighed and responded in positive. "Come on guys, speed up the work. Captain's getting angry."

Eighty minutes later, the internal comm. link rang up and the head reported "Captain, we have bypassed the fault and the ship's mobile. But please limit the speed to 25 knots while we are rectifying this issue." "Alright!!!" Amaira said and commanded, "Start the propellers. Limit speed to 25 knots."

Vivaan obliged but commented, "At this speed, we'll lose all our gains." "What is the distance between us and them?" Arman looked into his screen and responded, "Four ships approaching from south east 187.46 deg. Speed 30 to 35 knots, distance 35 nautical miles." The captain thought over the data, "They would cover the distance in about two hours. Prepare for battle, activate all defenses and put the armaments in full auto."

• • • •

THE JOINT CAPTAIN OF the interception fleet was informed, "Captain, we have spotted the ship. Still moving north at 20 to 25 knots, distance 34 nautical miles." The captain inquired, "Do you have any identification?" "Negative sir. We can now only determine the nature of ship with visual conformation." "How much time till we make visual contact with the ship?" "An hour at this rate."

The Chinese interceptors approached the Chanakya from starboard flank and at twenty six nautical miles got a visual sight of the ship, "Captain we have visual data and I am patching it through." The data operator announced and the screen in front of captain showed the ship. "It's an Indian ship..." The captain squinted to see the weapons and remarked, "It looks like a battleship."

The same feed was transmitted back to the control center. Admiral Wang giggled, "Well looks like India got a century back. Battleships are obsolete ships used more than a century ago, now you're trying to win against our revolutionary ships by these outdated ship designs." The entire staff laughed off and the admiral gave orders to the fleet to open fire once they get in range.

The distance between the two ships decreased to twenty five nautical miles when Chanakya opened fire first on the interceptors with its gigantic guns. "Captain, the Indian battleship has opened fire. Cruiser 17 has taken two hits and is signaling SOS."

"What? They disabled a cruiser with just two hits! All ships take evasive maneuvers. All ships will open fire once in firing range." The captain howled and all the interceptors scrambled and began to fire torpedoes and six inch shells as the distance reduced to fifteen nautical miles.

By that time however, much to the Chinese sailor's surprise the Chanakya took some serious hits to the enemies. Volleys after volleys of torpedoes were fired at the ship, "This should be enough to kill even an aircraft carrier." The captain said with a tinge of sadistic smile. A minute later when he was expecting a confirmation of a hit and possible crippling of the ship, the operator shouted "Captain, I have lost contact with the torpedoes."

"Did they hit?" He asked another officer who said, "No, contact detonation detected. Enemy ship seems all right." Before he can react, another shouted "Torpedo alert. Seven enemy torpedoes moving towards friendly ships at five meters depth."

"Take evasive action. All hands, brace for impact." An emergency alarm was sounded in the ships as the bridge maneuvered the ship haphazardly to avoid the torpedoes but to no avail as they hit the engines on the stern resulting in an explosion that killed everyone aboard. The entire battle – or rather the miracle lasted nearly thirty minutes.

3

INS Chanakya, the lone ship of Indian Navy's Eastern flank that escaped the Chinese incursion at Camorta Island; was now standing at a hundred nautical miles off the coast of Port Blair, the capital of the Union Territory of Andaman and Nicobar Islands.

"Damage Report." Captain Amaira announced into the intercom. "Three torpedo hits on the starboard armor. Hull integrity at 99%. Two armor plates compromised." "Begin damage control." She ordered as she put down the intercom receiver. "This ship can withstand quite a punishment." Amaira sighed.

"Captain, there is something we need to do about the short staff. I don't think we can fight a bigger fleet with such an understaffed ship." Naina said as she monitored all the systems one-by-one. Vivaan and Arman had taken leave to take rest after the intense fight. "I understand, but I think it would be best if everyone discusses it together."

Arman and Vivaan came to the bridge after an hour, "Good morning." It was four in the morning and the repairing work was nowhere close to finish. Amaira left as soon as the duo entered and Naina ordered, "Do a detailed scan of the surroundings and report in the strategy room."

The duo nodded and began scanning the surroundings using different equipment and tallied the data. The entire procedure took half an hour and then the duo proceeded to the strategy room. Amaira and Naina were already there, waiting for the duo.

"I called you here, because I feel there's an urgent issue that needs to be resolved." Naina began. "I feel that in current conditions we might not be able to fend off another attack by the Chinese." Amaira continued, "I agree with Commander Naina. Our repairs and maintenance is taking a lot of time, at this rate we'll just keep losing all the advantages we have in terms of firepower or speed. Moreover, the AI system just used twenty percent of the available ammunition."

"But captain, we have shrugged off the attackers once. I don't think we need to ask for any reinforcements." Vivaan interrupted and Arman added, "Moreover, in our state I don't think we can make to any Indian stronghold for reinforcements." The two ladies patiently listened to the points raised by the duo and answered, "We know that taking in reinforcements would be the last thing we'll be allowed."

Amaira continued as Naina paused, "So, I am proposing to draft the civilians into our ranks." Naina, Arman and Vivaan were perplexed by the decision. Arman began, "Well, it is not against the rules. It is clearly a power of captain that 'he/she shall recruit any willing civilian if the ship is in a distress and is carrying civilians.' So I think I'll support it."

Naina also came in support, "Civilian or not, every person aboard this ship has a responsibility to protect this ship. So I support the motion completely." Vivaan stayed silent, his silence showed his resistance to the idea. He simply went out of the room saying, "I'll inform you of my decision later."

Naina was annoyed by the answer and retorted, "Captain, this kind of behavior should not be tolerated in the ship. I propose disciplinary action against Lieutenant Vivaan immediately." Amaira however stayed calm and said, "Overruled!"

The members dispersed and went to their quarters. The monitoring systems were kept in automatic mode and the crew rested till six in the morning. Vivaan entered the bridge to see everyone waiting for him. Amaira stood up with a gentle smile, "So, what's your decision?" Vivaan was taken aback, "Why bother? You already are in a majority, so my vote doesn't count does it?"

"Well, I intend to take every decision unanimously. So if you're uncomfortable with the decision, we can look for an alternative." "No, there's no need. I think it would be better for us to have a fully crewed ship. I too agree." A cheer ran among the crew and Naina immediately announced the drafting procedure on the intercom.

"Attention all personnel aboard the ship. Due to the lack of crew aboard the ship, the Captain has decided to conduct a voluntary drafting of all civilians aboard the ship. Everyone above the age of fifteen is eligible for the procedure. Senior citizen, women with young children and people with disabilities will be exempted. I repeat..." All speakers aboard the ship relayed the message.

Within fifteen minutes, the drafting bench in the strategy room had a queue longer than those formed when anything new is released for free in India. 'This is the spirit that helped us endure this twenty month long war.' Amaira smiled as she saw Naina, Vivaan and Arman commit to their fullest.

The person who helped Amaira in the secret dock was taken as the main doctor and some ladies volunteered as nurses. Most of the men took technical jobs while ladies took work in the diners and other non-combat duties. This left the teenagers and early adults to take up the places in the bridge.

"Captain, they are all children. Do you think we need to draft them as well?" Vivaan asked Amaira who turned towards Naina and asked, "How many vacancies?" Naina pulled out a document and read, "We are yet to recruit for bridge and CIC. All others have been taken in technical duties and maintenance staff argued that they at least needed to be at full manpower."

Amaira sighed, "Yeah, maintenance team is required at full manpower. Okay continue with the process." Soon the remaining people were drafted. The repairing work sped up and the teenagers were given training in simulations.

January 18, 2040 – Chanakya's repair work finished at six in the evening, three hours after the drafting process was completed. An announcement was made "This is the captain of the Chanakya. The ship will leave in T minus 150, all crew members to proceed to their designated places."

All new crew members at the bridge had arrived except for one. "Who was the one recruited for the position of weapons control?" Amaira asked only to find a reply from the door, "I was." A teenager immediately ran inside the bridge and handed over her recruitment letter to Amaira.

She immediately recognized the girl as the one who shot the steam pipe back in Camorta. "Is she even fifteen?" Vivaan asked looking at the girl who didn't seem to be old enough. Naina pulled out her details and began, "According to records, she turned fifteen yesterday." The entire bridge looked upon the youngest member among them.

"Okay. All hands to their designated positions. You know what to do, increase the ship's speed to maximum in 600. Head northwards, CIC to switch to primary and radars to scan full area. Proceed cautiously." Amaira ordered and everyone immediately took their seats. "Radars all clear." "Nothing on SONAR." Ananya asked to Divya who was sitting next to her, "What do I have to say?"

Divya looked at her console perplexed and replied, "I don't know, there was nothing this complex in the simulations." Naina looked upon the duo and sighed at their immaturity, 'At this rate, we'll sink even before an encounter.'

· · · ·

Camorta Control Center, Nicobar Islands

"ADMIRAL WANG, THAT was the final footage the Type 014 sent before being destroyed." The communication officer informed the admiral who sighed in disbelief. 'That battleship took out the interceptors, cruisers and destroyers all by itself. I don't believe it.'

"Bring me the map of the area." He commanded the officers, 'Those damn Indians. If I were not bound by the rules, I would've forced the admiral to spit out all secrets.' The rear admiral came in with the nautical map of the Indian Ocean Region and spread it across the table.

"Hmm...So this ship emerged here, sent SOS continuously and suddenly disappeared upon reaching this point." The rear admiral nodded in agreement, "Yes Sir, our search fleet encountered them here 75 nautical miles from the last signal and at a further seven nautical miles, they were sunk."

"What do we know about the armaments?" Rear admiral pulled out a file with some pictures and showed them to Wang. "Twelve large caliber guns aboard four turrets. Though unspecified, a total eight smaller caliber guns aboard four turrets have been spotted." "That's all? It looks quite decently armed though."

The rear admiral bit his lip and began, "Apologies sir, but we don't have confirmations on any other weapons." "Okay and what about the torpedoes that sunk our ships." "Still not clear sir. We are unable to identify any structure that could launch torpedoes from the ship." Wang was quite impressed by the concealment, the battleship had. "I am guessing that you won't have any idea how our torpedoes didn't hit them."

The rear admiral nodded in negative, "I am only expecting it to be a torpedo malfunction." Everyone in the room sighed. "Anyways, the ship was moving northwards right?" "Yes sir, maybe due to the extensive presence of our forces in the southern direction." "Yeah, no captain with their brains intact would try to maneuver a ship through enemy forces."

"Sir, I think they are trying to make it to here." The rear admiral's finger moved from Andaman to Gujarat. "If I were to bet where the ship would go, I'll place my money on here. The Indian Navy's Western flank's HQ – Porbandar Gujarat. That's the only Indian Navy's stronghold remaining." Wang quickly noted and asked, "It's very near to our base in Gwadar, why haven't we destroyed it."

The rear admiral immediately switched tabs to show records of some battles. "We have tried it twice but failed. Their shore fortifications are very strong, landing crafts didn't make in. Our ships were stopped about ten nautical miles from the shore because of the water levels. And then the defending ships just rained hell on us."

"So it was left alone?" "Yes sir, after two disastrous attempts it was left alone." Wang looked at a picture and asked, "How do Indian ships come and go in here?" The rear admiral replied, "We don't know, ships are traversing the patch where water level is supposedly very low. But when we tried to push through, our ships simply hit the ground."

"Indians!!!" Wang sighed. "Anyways that ship moved north and has to go to the Western part. How do you think they can go? Is there any inland canal?" "Not any that we know." He wasn't impressed by the rear admiral's response. "Send five submarines to stalk the ship. They are not to engage. Inform the Hambantota port to expect some guests. Have an assault fleet ready which will follow the ship when it passes through the Indira Parallel. They are to engage the ship along with the Hambantota fleet."

January 19, 2040: The newly assigned crew of Chanakya was trained extensively in the controls and the systems of the ships. The captain ordered a battle drill and an announcement was made on the ship, "This is a drill. All personnel report to their battlestations."

Within five minutes, all officers were in the bridge synchronizing and attacking enemy fleet formations in a simulation. After the simulation ended, Amaira ordered the ship to turn eastward and ordered the crew to begin the shifts in the bridge.

Amaira came on the deck and strolled about the place among the superstructures – turrets, missile launchers, CIWS etc. "You, what are you doing here?" She asked Ananya who emerged from behind a turret. Ananya hastily pulled off a salute which the Captain responded with one of her own. "There's no need to be so formal here. But you didn't answer me, what are you doing here?"

Ananya replied immediately, "I was here for a little walk." However Amaira couldn't ask anything as the alarm sounded on the ship. The duo rushed back to the bridge and Amaira asked for a status report. Naina began, "Five submarines spotted on the SONAR, Blue Delta 150."

They were given basic training regarding the call signs of the ship in order to fast track communication among the members. The color represented distance beginning with black ranging from zero to five nautical miles, red from five to ten nautical miles, orange from ten to twenty nautical miles, yellow from twenty to thirty five, green from thirty five to fifty and blue from fifty to sixty five.

The Greek letters indicate angle measured from the bow of ship in phases of thirty degrees in clockwise direction – alpha, beta, gamma, delta, zeta, theta, iota, lambda, pi, rho, sigma and omega. The number determined the number of seconds the signal took to come back.

"Anything other than that?" Amaira asked as Ananya took her place and began searching the subs using her special sniping equipment. "They are moving at twenty three knots, and initial estimates show old models of diesel-electric subs by the noise they make."

"How old?" "2010-2020 range models." Amaira thought and looked at the crew, "All hands to Level one battlestations. Prepare for anti-submarine warfare. Load all starboard torpedo launchers with long range torpedoes. Reduce speed to fifteen knots and turn the ship starboard forty."

Within minutes, the Chanakya was on high alert. The armory personnel loaded the starboard torpedo tubes and prepared the depth charges. The ship slowed down in order to get the subs in the range, everyone in the bridge on their edge to kill the subs before they can fire their torpedoes or anti ship missiles.

• • • •

IN THE BRIDGE OF THE Type 002 submarine, the captain was informed of the slowdown of the ship. "They are preparing for combat but with whom..." "They're turning starboard." "Look for any friendly forces in the area and inform them of the development. We'll continue to stalk them."

The distance between the submarines and the ships begin to lessen and as the distance was forty nautical miles, the captain ordered, "Turn the subs, starboard twenty." The five stalkers continued their supposed silent run completely unaware that they've been spotted.

• • • •

ABOARD THE BRIDGE OF the Chanakya, everyone waited anxiously as the CIC officer counted down till the Chinese sub was in range of the torpedo. Ananya shouted, "I have a lock, distance thirty five nautical miles, three torpedoes." Amaira wanted to wait, but it would be fruitless to do so. Upon nearing the ship the subs would know that they are to be fired upon, but at this range they can easily maneuver out of range.

But one thing was sure; the ship couldn't handle an assault from five submarines at once. "Fire torpedoes." She ordered Ananya who pulled the trigger switch. The torpedo tubes located beneath the waterline flooded and three torpedoes – missiles of certain death in terms of naval combat came out and sped towards the stalking submarines.

The captain must've noticed the torpedoes, as he took evasive maneuvers but continued to close the distance. The explosive charge of the torpedo activated as the distance between the torpedo and the Chanakya increased to twenty nautical miles.

Homing to their nearest submarine, the torpedoes detonated taking down the one they were supposed to. Three submarines disappeared from the hydro-acoustic map leaving two approaching them from the blind spots of the weaponry.

"Incoming, six torpedoes. From stern, depth six meters." Navya shouted who was managing the Hydro-acoustics. "Charge the Electro-Magnetic Pulse Generator and release at 70%." Naina ordered Divya who responded with a "Yes Mam."

The Electro-Magnetic Pulse or EMP Generator sprang to life and drew massive amount of energy from the four nuclear reactors and at 70% charge let out a devastating pulse that destroyed all electronic equipment in its way. Had the ship not been insulated completely, it would've required an electronic overhaul every time the generators were used.

The torpedoes de-activated as soon as they hit the pulse and simply sank to the bottom of the sea. The submarine captain upon knowing that the torpedoes didn't hit, ordered a fresh volley to be fired upon the ship. Again six torpedoes were launched – they'd guessed correctly that the torpedo tubes were mounted somewhere along the length of the ship, so attacking towards its bow or stern would be effective as they would be protected against the torpedoes.

"Six new torpedoes, depth hundred meters." "They are going for the keel, how much time till we can fire the EMP again." Amaira asked. "The cooling systems are working at full power. It'll take three minutes before we can begin charging." Divya responded.

Ananya was quietly listening to the conversation and as the captain was about to order an evasive maneuver, she spoke, "Captain please order the ship to turn 90 starboard and tilt it starboard." "What are you saying, officer?" Naina asked but Amaira cut her short, "We don't have time to debate. Turn the ship; starboard 90 and flood all starboard ballast tanks."

"Hope you can answer this later." Naina said as the ship tilted and turned sooner than anyone would've expected. The torpedoes went right below the ship without touching them. "I have a lock, firing torpedoes." Ananya said in the midst of the turn and fired four torpedoes when the tubes faced direct bottom of the sea.

The torpedoes fell towards the bottom when their navigation kicked in and guided them to the remaining submarines who never expected such a move. The torpedoes took their kill, adding five to the ships kill count. The CIC immediately verified the kills and Amaira ordered the ship to be stabilized immediately after the maneuver ended.

"Get out of the combat zone. Move northwards and stop for damage checks after getting into stable waters. Downgrade to Level 3 battlestations. Proceed at maximum battle speed with constant lookout." Amaira ordered. Naina looked over the corner of her eye towards Ananya. 'I can't believe she learnt everything so quickly. It's worth three years of training in the Naval Academy.' "Maybe first-hand experience and desperation are the best teachers." Amaira whispered in Naina's ears.

The Chanakya turned back northward and stopped for damage check after moving twenty nautical miles from the position. The bridge was almost empty, with only Naina, Navya, Arman and Vivaan present. "Navya, you should go and take some rest." She nodded and left the bridge leaving the three officers alone.

"Vivaan, Arman! I want your opinion regarding our weapons control officer." Naina began and the duo who was too indulged in their work took a pause and thought for a while. "Well, she's quite talented. I must say that." Vivaan commented and Arman added, "Yeah, I agree and not just that, she is a civilian."

"Don't you think she's too well trained to be a civilian?" Naina asked and Vivaan replied, "Well, you were the one who checked the documents. Did you find anything out of order?" Naina sighed, "Nothing on her part, but still..." "I think it would be better for us to leave this background verification on the higher ups when we reach Porbandar." Arman remarked.

"No, I disagree. If there's any doubt regarding any of the crew members, it should be dealt with immediately." Amaira entered the bridge most probably after overhearing the conversation. "We don't want to be disrespectful..." Vivaan began but Amaira cut him off, "This is my ship and I decided that all decisions here would be unanimous, so even if there's a fraction of doubt among us we must root it out."

She moved to the intercom mike and announced, "Weapons control officer Ananya Anand is to report in the strategy room. I repeat..." Ananya who was strolling on the deck heard the announcement and wondered, "What happened now."

She slowly walked towards the room wondering about what would be in there. She knocked the room twice and asked, "May I come in?" Five seconds later, a response came, "Come In!!!" She opened the door to find an empty room with five chairs arranged in the center as a circle. Four of them were occupied by the Navy officers.

"Take a seat, officer Ananya." Amaira said and Ananya quietly went and took the vacant chair. "Officer Ananya Anand, we acknowledge that you're the youngest civilian we enlisted during the drafting. However, there appears to be some discrepancies regarding your data." Naina began.

"This is just a preliminary inquiry. If the panel is satisfied with your inputs, this matter is closed right here. Still this conversation is being recorded in audio and video for any legal proceedings afterwards. You can choose to remain silent on any question you don't feel like answering but there may be consequences later." Vivaan continued. "Okay, I hope the rules are clear. Shall we?"

Ananya nodded in order to reply Amaira's question. "First things first, we would like to know your full name?" Amaira began while the other officers begin to note and verifying, "May I ask why this question? I thought I told my name correctly during the talk." "Well, you did. But because we don't know extent of the error, it becomes necessary to begin right from the start. So, what is your full name?"

Ananya tried her level best not to succumb under the immense pressure, "My full name is Ananya Anand."

"What is your family background?"

"I don't have a family."

"All right, what is your personal background?"

"I was a local student in Camorta. Before that, I took a transfer from Vishakhapatnam."

"You came here after taking a transfer from Vishakhapatnam? Any specific reasons?"

"…" Silence

"All right, did you take any prior military training?"

"No."

"Any shooting lessons?"

"No."

"Any special courses at school?"

"Yes, a two month self defense course."

"Anything other than that?"

"No."

"Then, would you mind explaining how you're able to manage the weapons so efficiently and how do know so well about the design of the ship."

"..." Silence

This time Amaira waited, this whole time nothing stuck her out of ordinary. But now, she couldn't help but feel something fishy about her. Ananya after a full minute of silence spoke, "Is it wrong?"

"Pardon?"

"Is it wrong to manage the weapons efficiently or to know the design capabilities of the ship?"

"No, it isn't. But still it's not expected from a civilian."

Ananya pulled out a bookmarked book from underneath her coat and handed it over to Amaira. "Chanakya Class Vessels – Training Guide, is this an instruction manual?"

"Yes. Maintenance crew chief Mr. Pradeep gave it to me the other day."

Amaira opened the bookmarked pages, went through it and closed the book before returning it to her. "So, you've gone through this guide."

"Yes."

"Is there anything else you want to add?"

"..." Silence

"Okay, the inquiry is hereby concluded. You may take some rest before next shift."

Ananya nodded and saluted Amaira as she got up and moved out. "So, what are your views on the issue?" Amaira asked the trio. "I didn't feel anything odd, but she clearly wasn't comfortable when you asked about her family."

"She said she doesn't have a family, does that mean she's an orphan. I never heard any charitable orphanages in Camorta." Vivaan added to Naina's observation. Arman continued, "Now that I think of it, she has left more blanks than she filled. I mean, she answered most of the question in just Yes/No format."

Amaira interrupted, "There are many things people are not willing to talk about. Remember that from her point of view, we're completely strangers. I do think that we should take some rest. I'll like to have your thoughts after that." She stood up and left the room. The officers returned to their quarters and took some rest.

Amaira walked to the deck and wandered around the place to find Ananya sitting next to a gun turret. She moved closer to the teenager to find her asleep. 'That's a strange place to sleep.' She wondered when she noticed a teardrop flowing down her cheek.

5

Camorta, Andaman and Nicobar Island

"**S**ir, the stalking submarines have been sunk." An officer rushed to the Admiral's private quarters aboard the Chinese Type 102 cruiser. "What happened?" "Sir, apparently they engaged the ship they were pursuing and..."

Admiral Wang sighed at the incompetence of his subordinates. "I thought I told them only to stalk...anyways, where was the attack?" The duo went to the war room and the officer showed him the location on a digital map.

"North Andaman Sea! That ship's quite fast I guess." He popped the images taken before and tried to compare the data with all relevant designs available with the Chinese. "It looks like a battleship but it's faster than a destroyer. What have these barbarians made?"

He panned the map in all directions to find any significant lead on the ship. Since the subs were destroyed, there was no way another reconnaissance party could catch up even if he dispatched one. Sighting something of a relief, he asked the officers "What happened to our long ranged communications?"

"The Indians have destroyed their comm. tower. Though we have built it back, we still don't have the access codes for their network." Wang rubbed his chin and contemplated, "What about our satellite or long range links?" "There is very little Chinese satellite coverage in this area. The last one passed around two hours ago, so I think the next one would pass..."

"In four hours. This isn't good, we have a rouge ship running around destroying our naval resources and we cannot even contact our bases to warn them." Wang kicked the table in frustration. "Admiral, all we can now do is to try and get as much information about the ship from the Indians."

The officers suggestion seemed good but Wang knew from his experience how much difficult it is to deal with Indians. Before volunteering in the Navy, Wang was an intelligence officer for the MSS and dealt with the supposed Indian interference in Tibetan Autonomous Region.

"They aren't opening their mouth. I know that." He hissed slowly. "Put all our bases in the Indian Ocean Region on high alert and order them to immediately sink any suspicious ships lurking nearby." The officer saluted the Admiral as he left the room, disgruntled.

· · · ·

ABOARD THE CHANAKYA, the four naval officers met in the strategy room to discuss their next course of action. "We are traversing the Andaman Sea and I think the best course of action would be to swivel around the Andaman and Nicobar Islands to get away into international waters." Naina said.

"What are your views?" Amaira asked Vivaan and Arman who seemed bit puzzled. "We came north to avoid their fleets awaiting us in the South and now we have to go through them." Arman sighed. Vivaan agreed to Naina's position, "But I think it's better to swivel around the islands. Their naval might would be more focused on the inside and we might get a better chance of escaping."

"But this would be a problem." Arman pointed to a small island a little north to their location. "The Coco Island. China owns a naval outpost here. Going from south would mean getting in range of their shore bound defenses and being stalked again by the ships and subs, north would mean going into Burmese waters."

"I have a way around, we could either slip in the shadows of night or..." Naina didn't need to continue her statement. It was now upto Amaira to take the decision as the captain. "Inform the bridge, we'll turn port 30 and then turn around near Coco Island to swivel around the Andaman and Nicobar Islands."

"Captain, about officer Ananya; are you satisfied with the inquiry?" Arman asked. Amaira thought for a while and replied, "No." "So what do you think we should do? We can confine her and interrogate her properly." Naina suggested. "I don't think we need to do this. Put her on taps, Executive Officer Naina you're allowed to go for a full interrogation if you find anything fishy."

The bridge was informed of the development and the course was corrected. Naina began to investigate more about their mysterious weapons control officer only to find that she didn't talk much to anyone on the ship. "She's quite withdrawn, is it because she wants to hide her identity?"

Naina continued her investigations as the ship stopped and took a break till the light was low enough to let them pass through. She prepared a report and submitted it to the captain. Amaira read out the report for other senior officers.

"She has very little communications with people on the ship. She has periodic visits to the doctor. But the doctor has refused to tell why she was on periodic visits. That seems quite strange though. Why the doctor of all people?" She wondered.

Naina added, "The doctor said that it is against the ethics of his profession. But he mentioned that there's nothing of worth in her background." Amaira thought for a while and replied, "I will meet him face-to-face." She got up and left the room with Naina following her.

The duo went to the infirmary where the doctor and two nurses were. They were volunteers, coming right after the ship sailed from Camorta. "Aah...It's the captain. So how is the dressing going?" Amaira replied, "Thanks Dr. Ram, it isn't aching but I think it has begun to swell."

Amaira took off the overcoat and sat on the chair in front of him, extending her right arm. The doctor pulled up the cuffs of her half sleeved T-shirt to reveal heavy bandage under it. He slowly undid the bandages to reveal two sterile blocks under them. He slowly removed the cotton and washed the wound with anti-septic.

"I want to know why Ananya visits you regularly." She asked as the procedure entered the most painful part. "I thought that I told the others that it's against my professional ethics." Amaira took a deep breath to overcome the pain and continue, "Yeah, but at least you can tell us something about her. Even if it is her problem or her background."

The doctor paused for a while and finally gave up, "Well she is taking prescribed anti-depressants, Zalephon and Modafilin. That's all I can tell you." The wound was cleaned and a new dressing was applied and he administered an injection near the wound. "That's local anesthesia, it'll help in pain relief."

Amaira pulled up her overcoat and muttered, "Thank You!!!" before leaving the infirmary. "She's depressed?" Naina asked and Amaira continued till they reached her cabin. Amaira slipped into a recliner chair and Naina took another chair. "I don't think she only takes anti-depressants. The other two medicines are normally used in long missions by all armed forces."

"You mean GO and NO-GO pills." Naina asked and Amaira responded in affirmative. Naina soon left the cabin as Amaira's anesthesia began its effect. Naina resisted her intuition to confine Ananya and interrogate her properly; she now only needed to observe her for any suspicion.

In the darkness of night about 2 in the morning, Chanakya quietly began to creep across the sea in order to bypass Chinese held Coco Island. "Captain, we are only twenty nautical miles away from the base, isn't it too close." Arman asked Amaira who answered, "We are in the middle of night, Direct sight would not expose us but radar would. We must go close enough so that radar exposure is minimum."

Suddenly, activity sprang up in the naval base. "Have they spotted us?" Vivaan exclaimed. "Can't say. All hands to level one battlestations.

Prepare for Anti-Shore, Anti-Ship and Anti-Submarine battle. All radars to full power; load launchers one through five with SR-BrahMos and six through nine with Dhanush. Prepare to fire broadside on the port." Amaira commanded.

The ship's weaponry sprung into action, the four big guns moved to face the shore on the port side of the ship. "Artillery status!!!" Naina commanded and Ananya began, "Four main 16 inch turrets, Four 8 inch turrets and Four 6 inch turrets in position. Ready to Fire."

Amaira wondered over their next course of action when Arman shouted, "Some ships have begun to move." Fearing another trap, Amaira ordered "Open Fire. Destroy the enemy outpost." All guns opened fired raining twelve 16 inch, eight 8 inch and sixteen 6 inch shells on the shore installations per salvo.

• • • •

"THE ENEMY BATTLESHIP has opened fire. We have the location at Orange Alpha, moving east." The operator shouted as the first salvo's hit the shore defenses. The commander smirked as he waited for the ship's captain to make any foolish decisions. "Return Fire!!! Take enemy strength in account."

The shore defenses opened fire and defending vessels began to move out when the operator shrieked. "Sir, the vessels can't go out." "What happened?" "The vessels have run aground near the mouth." The commander couldn't believe the words.

The Coco Island base was designed in such a way that all incoming and outgoing ships had to go through an opening in the doughnut-shaped island. This ensured good safety for all retreating ships and allowed for cover fire while the ships moved out during any interception.

"How did they find the locations of the submarine ports?" The commander yelled knowing he wouldn't get any satisfactory reply.

"Launch the squadrons and prepare the anti-ship missiles. That is only one ship, sink it." He ordered.

Seventeen aircrafts prepared to launch while another fifteen took off, following the command. Their orders were to sink a single battleship. "I have only seen them in movies, are they really powerful?" One of the pilots chatted in the waiting room. "Who knows? The Commander says that they are about a century old." A second pilot replied, while another one added, "Well, the internet says that they are big and sluggish ships only meant to carry out heavy artillery bombing on other slow ships."

The little piece of information relaxed the grim atmosphere before the news came. "The entire first squadron has been wiped out." The pilots and even the commander were surprised; they were the best Chinese warplanes. Meanwhile, the artillery shelling continued relentlessly on the shore installations, destroying many fortified structures.

"There is no way a single battleship can do that. We must be facing at least a fleet." The Commander barked, "Incoming missiles!!!" A warning flashed in the room just as it and the whole complex was blown up. Missiles hit the airfield and destroyed it as well, leaving no survivors.

· · · ·

Camorta, Andaman and Nicobar Island

ADMIRAL WANG SAW THE entire battle of Coco island and was equally surprised and disgusted at the ship's capability. "Admiral, I think we must think about the events. A single ship can never single-handedly do shore bombardment, missile launching, taking out entire aircraft squadrons and destroy key strategic locations in the base all at once. I too think that it's the work of a fleet and that too, a big one."

Wang sighed, "Based on the observation, anyone would agree but we know that it is just a single ship." He looked at the broadside picture of the ship captured by the first wave of ships. "They have excellent air-defense, missile launchers, multiple caliber guns and torpedo launchers."

He took an electronic marker and began to mark different parts of the ship. "Guns are quite visible. But the missile launchers and air defense?" The rear admiral asked and Wang responded, "Torpedo housing structures are undetectable, so I think they are here – below the waterline."

"Like submarines?" "Indeed!!! But missile launchers and air-defense are a bit tricky." The rear admiral tried to swivel the photo like a 3D model but couldn't. "What do we have from their systems?" Wang asked and shut the pictures.

He went to the control room and repeated the question, an officer stood up and answered, "Sir, we don't have anything on that particular battleship but there are these." He put some blueprints on the screen. "What are these blueprints?"

"We don't know sir, except they are ship designs. The text is in high level German." The officer replied. "Decipher it!" "Sorry sir, but right now it's impossible. We'll have to send these blueprints back to mainland to decipher them." Wang clicked his tongue in irritation, "Can you do anything...here?"

The officer looked down when another rose, "Sir, all I can speculate is that they are old warship designs." He played the blueprints in a slideshow and remarked with each picture, "This is an early destroyer – an imperial Japanese, this is a modern destroyer probably Russian. That one seems a cruiser, WW2 era and this is a modern cruiser probably American. These are aircraft carriers, probably Japanese and American."

The officer finally switched to the last two blueprints he got, "And these are battleships?" Wang asked and the officer nodded. "The battleships are probably German and American." "Transfer all the data…" Wang only began the statement when a mysterious progress bar appeared and then all the data vanished leaving behind a completely blank system.

"So they've erased all the data permanently." Wang wondered and the officer replied, "It seems so." Wang turned to the officer who found the data, "We're dealing with a battleship. I want the blueprint data of all American and German battleships. Match them with the data we have on our rogue ship."

• • • •

"THAT'S ENOUGH OF YOU. Even the naval officers don't know the secrets of an enemy naval base. How'd you know what are their strongholds and weak points?" Naina yelled thumping on the metallic table that separated her and Ananya. Behind her, Amaira, Vivaan and Arman were standing; witnessing the interrogation.

But Ananya didn't budge. It was five in the morning and after the ship steered clear of danger at 3 am, Naina forcibly escorted her to the brig and had been trying continuously to get information out of the teenager. Amaira stepped in, "I think everyone should take some rest. We'll continue at nine. Till then, please do think about your course of action." She said looking at the little teenager who sat on a chair making a headrest by her hands.

The four naval officers left the cell, leaving Ananya alone in the locked cell. The four officers paused at the stairs, "Captain, do you really think she's a spy?" Vivaan asked and Amaira responded, "I don't know. Coming to think of it, wouldn't it be strange that she's not trying to hide that."

"It is true, but it is also a fact that she knows too much. We should at least be sure about the source of the information. Maybe she's not a spy but the one who's giving her the information could be." Naina said. Arman however, stayed silent. "Lieutenant Arman, what are your views on this matter?" "I think I'll just wait for the outcome." He said slowly.

The officers returned to the cell, Naina took a deep breath and asked, "Weapons Control Officer Ananya, we know that you have a lot of information about the enemy forces and our ship. Just tell us who is providing you this information and this matter will be closed forever." But Ananya stayed silent.

The four officers took their turns to try and get her cooperation but failed. Arman then went to the corridor and called out the person who was standing outside. The doctor came in with a small briefcase. He sat on another chair and tried on his part to get her co-operation. Though Ananya was a little open to him, she didn't divulge any information.

"What would you do, if this case ends right here?" Dr. Ram asked and she responded, "Once we get back to land, I'll just disappear and perhaps start my life anew." The interrogators left the cell and stood right outside. "Now would you tell us why you were prescribing ati-depressants?"

Dr. Ram sighed, "Well, she's suffering from stress response syndrome. She must've seen or witnessed something traumatic. So those medications are prescribed so that the conditions don't escalate." The officers agreed, "War can be quite traumatic and the events could lead anyone..."

"So, what do you think should we use the medical method?" Amaira asked. "I think we should try once again, maybe after repeated persuasion she can give the information." Naina responded and went inside, starting up the conversation again. Everything went the same way again and frustrated, Naina pulled out her gun and pointed it towards her.

"Fine, let's do it the old way. You'll give me the answers to every question I ask or else..." Amaira and Vivaan tried to stop her but were in turn stopped by Arman. They watched as Naina threatened the teenager with life. Ananya however said in a low tone, "Fine...go on and kill me."

"What?" Everyone present there flinched. Ananya pointed her right index finger at her forehead. "I am dead either way. So it's better this way. Shoot me, there's no one to mourn me." Naina's hand trembled for a moment as she heard the words. Ananya seemed to notice it and got up, walking to the officer until the gun's barrel touched her forehead.

Naina had regained her composure and held the gun firmly in place. "Let's see whose resolve lasts longer. Shall we?" She stared directly into Naina's eyes, who increased the pressure on the trigger. After two minutes of stalemate, Naina withdrew her gun and went out.

The group reassembled outside and Amaira asked Naina, "Executive Officer Naina, would you mind providing an explanation for your actions?" Naina sighed and responded, "Well, like I said it's an old trick. People, mostly children are very protective about their life. So maybe..."

Arman deduced, "Now we know the reason why she was protecting the information so dearly. Well, Commander Naina's observation is correct somewhat." Amaira responded, "So that means, she's either under a direct life threat or..." "...Or there's another spy here and maybe she knows that." Arman added. "Do you think that she'll tell us who threatens her?"

"Based on the conversation we had. No!!!" Vivaan said. Amaira took all the inputs and turned to Dr. Ram "Doctor, you may proceed." The doctor nodded and went in. He opened his briefcase and pulled out a little syringe. "What is that?" She asked but he didn't respond. Ananya's calm face first showed signs of panic as the doctor overpowered her and injected the unknown liquid in the vein of neck.

"Stay calm or you'll hurt yourself." He said before picking up his briefcase and leaving. Ananya tried to get up but couldn't, the entire strength of her body seemed to be draining. She forced herself on her feet but stumbled immediately. Her struggle with her waning strength lasted for five minutes before she passed out.

She woke up after an unknown stretch of time, lying on the bed of her cell. "Was that a dream?" She tried to get up, but her vision was blurry and head felt heavier than ever. The door of her cell was wide open, but she couldn't figure out why.

She slowly rose to her two feet and began to walk across the room. Her body still felt weak and slow, 'What's happening.' She held the walls for support and walked out of the cell. The first place she visited was the deck, then the bridge and then the living quarters.

She wandered the whole ship finding nothing out of the ordinary. Except the four naval officers, no one suspected her and it didn't seem nothing out of ordinary. Though she tried to visit the officers, she couldn't make up her mind and thus abandoned the idea. Her mind was full of different thoughts and she found that she could neither focus on anything nor control herself properly.

The only thing she could think of was to go to sleep. She wandered back to the cell, only to find it locked indicating that she was indeed free now. She limped back to her bunk and slept like a log until the next dawn.

6

The Chanakya cruised south with relative ease after the battle of Coco Island. After stopping for minor repairs, the ship cruised at constant 35 knots and on the dawn of January 21, he crossed the parallel latitude of Camorta. The ship travelled twenty knots east of the Island clusters.

The ship was on Level 2 battlestations as the Chinese were occupying Camorta's control station and perhaps now tracked them using the Radars of the naval base. The entire crew was on toes as they tried to stealthily pass through the controlled waters.

The ship made through the waters, and the security level was decreased. "I don't believe we made it out so far undetected." Naina said to Captain Amaira. "Maybe they weren't observant enough." Vivaan added but Arman stopped the duo, "I think there's no need of theorizing about that. We made it out of the radar range and that should be enough."

The trio agreed to his point when Amaira shouted, "Come in!!!" Everyone turned towards the door as Ananya entered the room timidly. "May we know why you are here instead of your station?" Vivaan asked and Ananya took a deep breath perhaps restoring the self confidence.

"Captain, I think we need to talk." She said in a low voice. A wave of delight ran through the officers but Amaira asked, "About?" Ananya was surprised, but she knew she didn't have any choice. "I am ready to give you your answers."

The officers showed an expression of relief, but her next statement caused them to rethink. Ananya continued, "Actually, I am here for a trade. I'll give you your answers and you'll provide me mine." Amaira responded after a minute of deliberation, "OK!!! So you want to begin here or..." "No, it's fine here."

The five of them took a chair on the table. Ananya began, "I'll be really glad if you could please keep everything off-record." The officers looked at each other and then agreed. They already deduced the pressure the teen must've been. Amaira again began,

"So, everything that you told us in the previous meeting here was lie."

"No, it was part truth."

"You hid some information from us."

"Yes, I did."

"Would you mind telling the reason?"

"Out of fear."

"Fear! Do you mean you have done something that you shouldn't?"

"It depends on how you see it."

The officers were quite astonished by the speed and clarity of the answers. But they didn't interrupt and continued noting down the details.

"Okay, Let's start with your family background. How many family members you had?"

"Four."

"The name of your parents."

"My father was Mr. Gautam Anand and my mother was Mrs. Sarita Anand."

"You mentioned 'was', so does that mean - ?"

"Yes, they are dead. My elder brother Sadashiv Anand is also dead."

The information itself had gruesome weights. 'No wonder why she was so much withdrawn.' Naina wrote as a side-note. 'That's why she was taking the anti depressants. Anyone who lost their entire family is indeed going to be in a serious depression state.' Amaira thought as she put forward the next question.

"You can remain silent if you want on this one but how did they die?"

"My brother was a crew member of the ship destroyed in the Malacca Disaster. Even though he survived the torpedo explosion, he was killed when those bastards opened fire their machine guns on them."

"And your parents?"

"They were killed on the attack on Camorta, right in front of me."

The officers gasped in horror as she continued, "My parents were in the next bunker; we were separated because they pushed me first in that bunker and sought shelter in the other one. Remember Captain, when you led us out of the complex we saw them killing the inhabitants of the other bunker..."

"Were they in...?"

"Yes."

"How did you get all the data regarding the naval capabilities, strongholds and weak points of the Chinese military?"

Ananya hesitated for a moment before reaching out for her pocket and pulling out a memory chip. "This is the only thing I've as a legacy from my parents." Amaira took a look at the chip but didn't run it. "Oh, I see." She said before returning the chip to Ananya.

"How did your parents get their hands on the information?" Naina inquired.

"Officially, my parents were enlisted as investigative officers under the Joint Military Wing. But actually, they were infiltrators. They used to scout different bases in the Indian Ocean Region and collected data on various ships, plans and even the base itself."

"They never got caught?"

"No, from the stories they used to tell – they used a civilian boat to do everything and mostly on or after a stormy day. Dad used to do all the talking, while mom snuck up all the data."

"About your combat training?"

"Officially, I only had a two month self defense course. But mom and dad taught me all infiltration techniques and trained me to expert level."

"What do you mean?"

"Um...to put it numerically, I was trained by them for five years in hand-to-hand combat, propaganda, weapons combat, martial arts, ethical and unethical hacking, sniping, assassination and tactical distraction."

"You can't be serious!!!" Vivaan and Arman exclaimed. "You can go on and test it." Ananya challenged the duo. 'She wouldn't tell lie, not at this point.' Arman thought and refrained from taking up the challenge. But Vivaan didn't even think twice before yelling, "Fine, I'll see that myself." Ananya and Vivaan stood from their chair and went aside for their challenge. Amaira, Naina and Arman watched as the two begun their brawl.

Ananya stood in front of Vivaan who immediately pounced on her. Seeing the officer coming rushing to her, Ananya braced herself for the attack. She pulled up her hands close to herself and took the first hit. 'He's tough' She almost yelped as she stumbled backwards due to the force.

"Huh, you're a lousy fighter. Five years of training? Even a kid can do better." Vivaan barked but Ananya smirked in response, maintaining her defensive posture. Vivaan charged again, this time he used a full body-shoulder slam.

Ananya waited till the last moment and then dodged the charge, stabbing Vivaan's mid-rib by the elbow and grabbing one of his arms. Vivaan forced his arm out but it was too late, Ananya's free arm hit him at the base of his skull; rendering him unconscious.

The doctor was called who nursed Ananya's little wounds and brought Vivaan back to consciousness. After tending the duo, Dr. Ram asked Amaira for a private talk. Naina and Arman looked at the beat-up Vivaan who was comforting his injured arm. "Sorry Lieutenant, but that must've hurt a lot." Naina burst into laughter after being unable to control it.

Vivaan grumbled, "I never thought, she would be such a trained soldier." Naina teased, "She's not a soldier; she is an infiltrator albeit an unofficial one." Amaira returned after having a talk with Dr. Ram. "Sorry for the delay. So Lieutenant, I do hope you had your doubts cleared."

Vivaan nodded painfully. "So, continuing on. I want to know from you, Weapons Control Officer Ananya. What did you fear that you hid the information?" Ananya looked around and whispered in a barely audible tone. "I think there's another infiltrator on this ship, someone from the enemy side."

"What?" A common statement emerged from the four officers. "Do you even know what are you pointing at?" Naina asked and she replied, "Yes, I am also an infiltrator and none of you knew that before I began to exploit my knowledge. I am pretty sure there is another, no...there must be another."

"Is there any specific reason for your suspicion?" Amaira asked. "Yes, I have been observing the events around the ship constantly and have seen many sabotage attempts. So..." "We did think about that. But even if we know there's a spy around here, how are we supposed to know who is it?"

"We can think of that in the next strategic meeting. But now, for our side of the bargain, what do you want to ask us?" Ananya looked straight into Amaira's eyes, "I want to know what happened the other day? What was that thing which he injected into my neck?"

Amaira had already guessed her demand, so she brought out a video clip and played it on a screen. It showed from the moment Dr. Ram injected the mysterious liquid in her neck and her struggle till she fainted. "You must know this part, do you?" Amaira asked and she nodded. Amaira then continued the video:

· · · ·

DR. RAM CAME IN AFTER a few minutes and noted her pulse. "There seems to be no side-effects for now. You better finish it in fifteen minutes." Vivaan and Arman carried her to the bed of the cell and pulled the five chairs near her.

The doctor continuously monitored her pulse while the officers began to ask questions one-by-one, while she answered them in a very broken and almost incomprehensible tone.

"What is your name?"

"A...na...ya"

"Where did you live?"

"Ca...mo...ta"

"Where did you get the information?"

"I...I...in...for...at...on"

"It is becoming more and more incomprehensible." Naina complained and Dr. Ram said quickly, "She is passing from twilight stage to semi unconscious state. Ask whatever you want but do it fast, if she transitions to total unconscious state it would be very difficult to bring her back."

"Who is the spy, Ananya?"

"Spy...Spy...S..."

"Who gave you the information? Is that person on the ship?"

...Silence...

"Are you here, Ananya? Can you hear us?"

...Silence...

Dr. Ram was alarmed and immediately called a halt. He immediately injected another liquid into her arm and stood up. "Sorry officers, but any further would cause irreversible harm to her body and psyche." The doctor and the officers left the cell leaving her unconscious there.

. . . .

"YOU DO KNOW WHAT HAPPENED after you came back to consciousness." Vivaan said. Ananya nodded in response and added, "What were in those injections?" Dr. Ram entered the room and responded, "That was SPDM, a chemical that comes under PDM – a sub-class of general anesthesia. Under proper dosage, it renders the target in full comatose state in seconds."

"You gave me that?" Ananya asked, her expression showing a rare hint of disgust. "Nah...Actually, I gave you just 0.07% of the proper dose. You passed out after five minutes of struggle and remained in twilight zone for about seven minutes before you slipped into semi comatose state."

"And why was I giving out those random words?" "Well, they weren't random words. In twilight zone, your active conscious was at minimal activity. Therefore, you weren't able to think anything; so those words were the first thing that came into your mind when you heard the questions."

"What was the second injection?" "That was the antidote. You see, PDMs are very stable in themselves and human body is incapable of flushing them out of bloodstream. So, an external agent is used to destabilize it, so that body can flush it out." Ram ended his explanation, being wary of Ananya who showed clear signs of displeasure. Ananya stood up from the chair and began to exit towards the door when Naina announced, "Weapons Control Officer Ananya, from now on your presence is required in every strategic meeting."

7

The evening of January 21, the Chanakya sailed through the now treacherous waters of the Indian Ocean. He sailed southwards to avoid getting caught in the Chinese stronghold of Sri Lanka. The ship was at Level 3 Battlestations, but constant vigilance was kept around.

The bridge had five members – Ananya, Naina, Vivaan, Ayush and Kavya. The bridge crew worked in shifts of twelve hour each, with two trained Navy members always on the bridge. Suddenly, Ananya shouted in alarm, "Mam, I have a silhouette in the targeting sensor."

The whole bridge was alerted and Naina ordered, "What's the status on Radar and Sonar?" "Nothing!" The response came. Naina went over to Ananya's station and looked at her screen. There was nothing, it was completely blank until Ananya pointed to a certain part of the screen.

"Switch it to night vision." Naina ordered and the scene became a bit clearer. It was the mast of a warship for certain, "It's not on the radar. What is the distance?" Ananya responded, "About 270 nautical miles." "That's over 500 km. That's why we aren't able to see it in the radar. Stop the ship immediately while we're still outside their range,"

The ship was brought to a halt and the bridge crew discussed the matter. Dr. Ram had given strict warning to Amaira along with sleep medications to help her recover from the gunshot wound. "We encountered this situation in the absence of the captain. The worst part is, we can't disturb her now." Naina sighed.

Vivaan thought for a while and added, "Do you think it's a Chinese ship?" Ananya nodded in negative, "No clue. The only thing on seeing them feels like those three are waiting for something. We don't have their broadside facing us." Naina looked at all her options and responded, "Weapons Control Officer Ananya, can you take them out?"

Ananya immediately responded in a 'yes' and added, "I'll require three shots." The officers returned to their stations and the ship's condition was upgraded to Level – 2 battlestations. "Activate Ultra Long range guns." Naina ordered.

"Converting all 16 inch guns on turret one to ultra long range mode. Beginning capacitor charging." Ananya exclaimed and everyone looked at the targeting system, Ananya patched to the screen. On the outside, the gun barrels split into two semi-circular cylinders and two long rails emerged from the turret and extended way beyond the length of the turret.

All the vents of the ship opened as the nuclear reactor's output soared to power the giant capacitors encased in thick armor just below the turrets. The capacitors charged to 100% in about five minutes and as the charging completed, Ananya said "Capacitors charged. Ready to snipe the unknown ships. Your orders commander."

Naina took a deep breath and replied, "Open Fire!" Ananya pulled the trigger; the massive capacitors discharged immediately forcing a large amount of energy into the rails and hence into the armor piercing warhead that sped towards the unknown ships at Mach 10. Three shots were fired from the front turret one within one minute and the bridge waited to get the results.

In normal warships, shell accuracy depended solely on luck. But the Chanakya had a special calculation system that took into account all local factors like relative velocity, wind movement, enemy' tendency to turn and the distance between the two ships to give near accurate results. Two minutes have passed since the first shot was fired but the screen showed nothing.

"Did they hit?" Kavya asked. No one answered, and everyone just looked at the stationary warships and waited for any hint of impact. About twenty seconds later, an explosion rocked on the stationary ship and within minutes two more on other ships. The unknown ships rocked under the impact and began to capsize.

"What happened?" Amaira asked as she entered the bridge moments after the feed was cut. The entire crew stood up and saluted Amaira who hastily put her uniform and rushed to the bridge immediately when the sound of the guns firing woke her up. "Executive Officer Naina, would you explain why we fired without calling for a Level one Battlestations."

Naina came forwards and answered in a crisp tone, "Weapons Control Officer Ananya spotted an unknown warship on her equipment. We were outside radar range, but owing to our proximity to Hambantota port; it could've been a Chinese Ambush. So I took the liberty of ordering their sinking using our main guns."

Amaira nodded as it was the course of action she would've taken. "Start the propellers, turn port. We'll take a detour by a hundred nautical miles southwards and approach the shipwreck for a rescue operation." Vivaan and Ananya interrupted in unison, "But Captain, they're enemies."

"That's right. But we don't know anything about them, it could very well be a friendly ship. Even if they are Chinese, we can take them as prisoners of war." Amaira responded and took her position as the captain. The quad propellers began to rotate and the ship steered port.

About eight hours later nearly at 11, the Chanakya reached the site of shipwreck. Navigating through the debris, the spotters finally managed to spot two life rafts. The deck crew through a lifebuoy and pulled the men onboard.

The twelve men stood on the deck with varying clothes. Some had blue camouflage dress underneath the white life-jacket while some wore a white one. Only one of them, perhaps the most senior one had a black overcoat. All of them had small firearms in the holster of their uniform.

Amaira, Naina, Vivaan and Arman came to the deck, and the deck crew stepped aside to provide them the way. The officers immediately identified them as non-Chinese but pretended otherwise. "Are you Chinese, sailors?" Amaira asked the men.

The rescued men didn't answer and looked at each other for some time, knowing that their rescuers might not be friendly at all. The sailor wearing the black coat came forward, "We want to know your affiliation. Which country does this battleship belong to?"

Amaira announced, "You are standing on the deck of an Indian ship, INS Chanakya. Now, tell us about your affiliation. Which country do you serve?" She pulled out her gun and pointed it towards the man. The man eased up and replied, "My name is Lieutenant Commander Andrew Gibbs. We are the last remains of the third scouting fleet of the US Navy."

Amaira looked at the men by the corner of her eye and withdrew her gun. "Take them to the infirmary. Have Dr. Ram examine all of them." The Americans were taken to infirmary and Amaira reached out for the wireless communicator in her ear. "Weapons Control Officer Ananya, report immediately in the Strategic room."

Ananya, who was stationed at the stern of the ship, responded in affirmative and packed the giant sniper rifle. The Armory in-charge took the heavy rifle from her and returned it to the ship's inventory. Ananya immediately headed to the strategy room where she was met with a furious Amaira.

"Do you have any idea which ship you've attacked?" She first asked. "That was a non-Chinese ship." The response shocked Naina and Vivaan who were present on the bridge. "You knew all along?" "It depends on how you see it."

Amaira shouted, "I don't want to hear your philosophy. As the captain, I want an explanation." Ananya began, "There were only three ships; though they can take out any ship easily if they possess missiles but given our previous encounters, I highly doubted that they would let only three ships attack us."

"Couldn't you have told us back then?" Vivaan asked. "No, it was a doubt, not a surety. I thought it would be better if we stayed clear of any suspicious warships." Ananya replied. Amaira sighed, "Do you know the consequences of your actions? You could be sentenced to death for this."

"What did this little girl do to draw death sentence?" The American sailor who introduced himself as Andrew Gibbs entered the room exchanging a quick formal salute with the captain. "So what happened?" Naina stammered, "Actually she..." But she stopped as Ananya spoke, "I forgot to tell the captain that a small ship exited our radar visibility range."

The four Indian officers controlled themselves from exclaiming realizing that she was lying. The lieutenant smiled and sat on a knee, holding her chin "Do you know which kind of ship was it." "A small warship, probably a frigate or missile boat. It went towards starboard at 70 degrees."

"You know, kid. I have a daughter; she is almost the same age as you. You don't belong on a warship, so why are you here?" Ananya returned his compassion and answered, "This ship belongs to my country and it's my duty to protect the others here. If you'll excuse me..."

Ananya left the room and the lieutenant turned towards the navy officers. "Who is she?" "Her name is Ananya and she is weapons control officer of this ship." Naina responded. "But isn't she too young to be an officer." Vivaan added, "She isn't trained. She was drafted a few days back."

The lieutenant was shocked, but didn't lose his cool "Wait, you had to draft a teenager, were you that much understaffed?" "Except for us and a few technical team members, all of the crew comprises only of civilians." The lieutenant wanted to lecture them on moralities but refrained. "Captain Amaira, as a gesture of gratitude we would like to help you on this ship till we get to an Indian Naval stronghold."

Amaira thought for a while and replied, "Ok, you are authorized to go anywhere on this ship except for the bridge and CIC. They are off-limits." Andrew smiled and left the room.

8

Early morning of January 22, Ananya's vigilance shift was over and she was taking some rest when an alarm ran on the ship, "This is the captain, we have encountered a hostile fleet. All hands to Level One Battlestations, I repeat..."

She quickly grabbed her dress and rushed to the bridge. Taking her seat next to Divya, she asked "What happened?" Divya responded as briefly as possible. "We were spotted by some Chinese ships and they have opened fire on us."

Amaira cut short their gossip and yelled, "Prepare anti ship missiles in launchers one through five. What is the artillery status?" Ananya immediately replied, "Loading launchers one through five with Anti-ship missiles. Artillery will be ready to fire in ten seconds."

"Incoming missiles, six of them." Divya shouted. "EMP?" Naina asked, "Negative, still under cooling phase." "Shoot them down with CIWS." All deck based CIWS sprang to life, sprinkling 12 mm bullets on the missiles detonating them prematurely.

· · · ·

ABOARD THE CHINESE flagship, the commander ordered the twelve frigates to keep up the missile barrage, while seven destroyers snuck up to the enemy ship to sink it with torpedoes. "Sir, frigates one through six are reloading." An officer said. "Okay order frigates seven through twelve to begin firing. Don't let the battleship get into firing range. What happened to the backup forces."

"They are reporting issues with their supply vessel. It'll take them two hours to reach here." The officer replied. "Sir, the ship is moving forward with great speed. Distance 70 knots and closing." Another officer remarked. "What about our submarines?" "No signal sir." The captain gritted his teeth and asked, "Destroyers?" "They were sunk by the main turret fire of the enemy ship. Single shot."

"Wait shells are not so effective. Are you sure." The officer played a clip recorded by a scouting plane. The destroyers snuck up to the port and starboard flanks of the ship and were about to fire when the turrets moved with incredible speed and shot them down. "You got to be kidding me!!" He exclaimed.

"Sir the ship has entered its firing range and has begun to fire on our frigates and corvettes." Another officer shouted. "They're prioritizing small ships over heavy cruisers. What does the captain intent to do? How much time till they last fired?" "Sir ten to twelve seconds."

The commander had a smile on his face and responded, "A battleship's main guns take time to reload, we'll sink them after the next salvo." He waited as the Chanakya fired the next rounds and ordered, "All ships move closer. Sink it within forty seconds." All the remaining ships moved towards the Chanakya and began to fire on it.

However within ten seconds, the Chanakya's primary and secondary turrets rotated facing the ships and opened fire, critically damaging the ships leaving them as a floating wreck.

• • • •

THE BRIDGE CREW COMMEMORATED the fall of the enemies when Naina reminded them, "It's not over yet. Prepare for phase two." The bridge crew went to the deck where they met with the Americans and the armory crew. The Armory in-charge handed Naina a large gun with a few grappling hooks.

Naina fired the first hook which anchored on the destroyed superstructure of the warship. Amaira turned towards Ananya, "There might be soldiers on deck. Be wary of them." Ananya nodded and whispered to Divya. "I want you to go to my station, fingers on the trigger. If anything suspicious happens, shoot all warships." Divya nodded and left.

Using a safety hook attached to her life-jacket, Ananya jumped off the deck towards the enemy warship. Upon reaching half-way, a second line was fired just beneath her and the armory master along with the Americans following him.

It was decided in the previous strategic meeting that their ammunition were ending faster than expected and hence they should limit the damages done to enemy ships and instead use their ammunition. Since, all naval ammunitions were standard type due to the Treaty of Singapore their ammunition usage will be limited only by the caliber of the guns.

Ananya neared the warship when she got caught in a suppressive fire of bullets. "Captain, what are these bullets coming from." She swung around to avoid the spray of bullets whose accuracy and precision were way below expectations. "It's CIWS fire, but since the control was destroyed it must be in manual mode. Keep swinging, they won't be able to hit you."

Ananya struggled with her maneuvers and replied, "It's easier said than done." As she reached the last few meters, she unbuckled the hook and took a free fall towards the deck. She landed on all fours near a CIWS gun manned by two Chinese soldiers. They said something to each other and picked up their rifles but were struck hard by Ananya who took their weapons as well.

Ananya moved around the deck in order to find anyone foolish enough to attack her. Though some tried, she made quick work of them by shooting them in the head. The whole team met at the deck and venture inside the ship.

Though the rest of them are confused over the layout of the ship, Ananya easily navigated through the unknown ship. She stopped in a corridor for sometime looking at the two exits. "What happened? You lost the way?" Andrew asked. "No, I was just wondering where can we get most of the resources. Bow magazine or aft magazine."

The lieutenant smiled and ordered, "We'll form two teams, one will go to the aft magazine in the right and take any resources they see fit. I and this little lady will be in the other team and go to the bow magazine in the left." The fourteen member team was divided into two seven member teams and went as planned.

Ananya and the lieutenant walked for some time when someone seized the girl from behind and shouted, "FREEZE!!!" The team instantly turned around to find a Chinese sailor, probably high-ranking officer grabbed Ananya by the neck. The teenager gasped for air while he asked, "What are you doing here?" No one answered and a little squeak emerged from Ananya's throat, "Scavenging."

"You're the talking one. Now you all, put down your weapons and surrender or else who knows what harm may come upon this little girl." The six of them began to activate the safeties of their weapons when Ananya's struggle seized, her eyes rolled here and there and closed.

The officer knowing that he could lose his bargaining chip loosens his grip in order to let her breathe. Suddenly, "BANG!!!!" a very hard surface hit his nose and it began bleeding. He looked down to find the girl who supposedly lost consciousness standing right in front of him, perfectly all right.

"You~!!!" He cursed as he drew his handgun and it towards her. "I'll kill you!!!" "Oh really, without these?" Ananya showed the frustrated sailor a magazine which she managed to extract from his gun while he grappled her tightly. But the man gave a wicked smile and said, "There's still one bullet left and I won't miss." And he pulled the trigger.

Ananya immediately responded by throwing the magazine towards the gun. But she was a bit late, the magazine didn't hit the gun to make the shot miss but rather the bullet pierced the magazine holder and a bullet shell causing the magazine to explode right on his face.

The explosion killed the Chinese man but due to being at some distance, Ananya was spared with just some shrapnel protrusions and mild burns. The team went to the magazine and used the feeder crane to pull out the 8 inch armor piercing and high explosive shells along with some missiles.

The other team got their hands on a plethora of anti ship missiles and torpedoes. The ammunitions were sent back through the cables and the team came back as well. Though everyone wanted Ananya to rest owing to her injury, Amaira had to send her in following raid missions as only she knew the interior of Chinese ships.

The other raid missions were successful and they got quite an arsenal of weaponry. "There's a problem captain." Amory In-charge exclaimed. Amaira asked about the problem and he replied, "We are unable to get ammunition for our main guns." "Even though she uses them effectively, they are our go-to weapons for long range attacks." Amaira said.

Meanwhile, Ananya was taken to the infirmary to have the shrapnel removed from her body. The doctor conducted a two hour surgical removal, following which she was advised bed-rest. Dr. Ram went to the strategic room where the four officers and the American lieutenant discussed their next plan.

He knocked at the open door twice and entered the room. "Captain, this is her medical report. I have removed twelve pieces of shrapnel from her body. There are some more in relatively non-lethal parts that would need surgery later." He reported handing over the file to Amaira.

"Why didn't you remove them now?" Vivaan asked. "The places where the shrapnel pieces penetrated require mitigating through some major arteries. It would take a lot of time and resources to conduct such a surgery." The doctor answered and Naina added, "Something we are running short on."

"Will she be able to man her station?" Amaira asked drawing everyone's resentment. "Well...yes, she can. But I'll recommend letting her get as much rest as possible. She has already lost quite an amount of blood." Naina asked, "Captain would you mind telling why she should be in battle with such injury?"

"Yeah, you even had her go to other raid missions despite having shrapnel injuries." Andrew asked. Amaira looked at all of them one at a time and responded, "One, we don't have any spare personnel and weapons are the most important asset we can have in battle. Two, only she has managed to learn the layout of all Chinese ships based on our intelligence reports."

"Well, we can man the weapons station. We're twelve and well trained in naval combat." Andrew suggested and Amaira gave him a sour look and said, "The meeting's dismissed." Everyone left one-by-one leaving Andrew behind who kicked the table in frustration and left the room.

He went to the deck, frustration reflecting on his face. His subordinates met him there and asked, "What happened Commander, any success?" Andrew replied, "No, Max. The captain won't let anyone of us even wander near the bridge." The entire group wandered on the deck discussing something when they stopped abruptly.

The group saw Ananya, sitting underneath a gun turret. "Is she asleep?" A soldier wondered and went close, looking at her bandaged face when she suddenly opened her eyes. Before the sailor could move, she grabbed him by the collar and threw him against the heavily armored gun turret.

"Ouch..." He mumbled when he saw the weapon in her hand. It was a combat knife – American made. "My knife..." He looked at the holster to find the knife missing, apparently she pulled it out when she threw him. Holding the knife by the blade, Ananya threw it towards the soldier who dodged it purely by instinct.

"Stop it. He's one of my men little miss. Joe, who asked you to disturb her. Don't you see she's injured?" Andrew shouted and Joe who had his eyes shut tightly opened them to find his hair cropped by the flying knife. He gave a sigh of relief, "She was injured? I don't what she would've done if she'd been all right."

Max exclaimed, "Whoa, she's tough fighter." "You weren't in the team that went to the bow magazine. That's why you're surprised." Another man said. "Men, get back to your positions. Kid we need to talk a bit." The group dispersed leaving the two of them alone near the turret.

"How are your injuries?" He asked. "I am fine, though it hurts a bit." She replied pointing towards her chest where most of the shrapnel hit as she protected most of her face by arms leaving the mid-section wide open. "So why don't you let anyone of us handle your battlestation for a while and take some rest."

The little girl thought for a while and replied, "The captain won't allow it." Andrew thought for a while, 'It is almost same as I thought.' "Do you know why your captain doesn't want us near the bridge? We help her in many ways." Ananya walked to the railing of the ship and replied, "It's not just the captain. If I were in her shoes, I would've done the same."

The response left Andrew shocked as he wondered, 'She enjoys immense loyalty from her sailors. I'd never even imagine this happening to me.' "And why would that be?" She turned around looking into Andrew's face, eye-to-eye. "We are twenty months into the war, and what kind of assistance have you given us. America has always treated us like we were the aggressors. Since your deal with China relating Taiwan has concluded, your forces have left the entire Indo-Pacific. Not bothering what that giant would do."

"It's not true, we still have bases in the IOR and..." He tried to justify when she snapped in between, "You should try that on someone else not me. I can easily look through your lies. Your nation forgot all promises it made on security, the quad, the data sharing and what not. Even when they captured large parts of our country, your country issued statements asking India to stay calm and accept a ceasefire."

"But you didn't. Listen you don't know anything about diplomacy, entire countries and wars can be won through diplomacy. We were just advising you to get that sorted out with diplomacy." Ananya listened to the soldier and laughed, "Like you won in Vietnam or Afghanistan. Or may be Iraq, Libya or Syria. The whole crew suspects that your ship wasn't sunk by the Chinese, you've scuttled your own ship and within a month or two some American Engineers would come here and get the ship back up."

Another sailor came, probably he heard Ananya's complaints. "We lost hundreds of men in those three shipwrecks and you think we staged all this." She replied with no sympathy, "Everyone aboard this ship is sure of that, even you twelve must know that." At that very moment, siren ran through the ship "This is your Captain, we have detected hostile enemy fleet pursuing us. We'll be entering combat in T minus 600. All hands to Level One Battlestations."

Ananya turned and walked away from the astonished Americans. Andrew was left perplexed, as the words ran through loops in his mind. A screech broke away his chain of thoughts. His fellow sailor jumped upon the girl, with his combat knife. "You'll be sorry for that insult." He yelled as he ran towards her.

Out of nowhere, she ducked creating an obstacle over which the attacker tripped and lost his balance. "Whoaa…" He cried as he fell but stopped short of hitting the ground. Ananya pulled him up with a jerk and tossed him towards the railing. He gained sense to find his knife gone and Ananya approached him, her face devoid of all emotions.

She pulled him up by the neck and held him right above the edge. "I don't know what reasons the Captain has to let you onboard. But I'll tell you one thing; I don't mind throwing the twelve of you as fodder for aquatic animals." She said as Andrew watched her, frozen in horror. She released the sailor who fell down towards the water.

Andrew jumped from his position, his instinct telling him to shoot Ananya right in the head. 'No, I must save him first.' He looked over the railing to find the sailor lying on a lifeboat. He pulled him out using a near-by rope. "Commander..." The sailor said totally astonished as how a little teenager almost killed him in cold blood.

The American crew re-assembled where the incident was discussed. "That girl did this, I don't believe it." Said another sailor. Joe however said, "I do believe it. Her strength is way beyond her looks. I know how she played with me like a rag-doll." Max was enraged by the comments and responded, "How insensitive could she be? We sabotaged our ship to get here – on this inferior battleship!!!"

At that moment, all main guns fired broadside on the enemies. The sailors took up their binoculars and viewed as seven fast destroyers were sunk, "Seven destroyers in a single salvo?" One sailor yelped. "And that's at seventeen nautical miles." Another added. Before another one could add their valuable input, the main guns trained again and fired another broadside.

"You'll have to admit one thing men. Neither is this an ordinary battleship, nor does it have an ordinary crew." Andrew remarked as the salvo took out many of the remaining ships. "I disagree commander; this is just a tech-up battleship. It's a century old design; one Tomahawk is enough to blow this thing to ribs." A sailor added, and Andrew replied "No, this thing has enough power to sink the entire seventh fleet before they can even detect it. I can tell this by experience and don't forget that only an untrained teenager is manning the weapons station."

9

"So you have a complaint of Weapon Control Officer Ananya manhandling one of your sailors." Amaira asked and Andrew replied in affirmative. The rest of the people including Naina, Vivaan, Arman, Divya and Kavya stifled their giggles. 'They would never believe that such a small girl could do that. Those guys...' Andrew cursed his crewmates while Amaira replied, "All right, I'll ask her to mend her behavior. But on an off-record comment do you think you might've just imagined things."

Andrew came out of the captain's room and sighed, "Maybe I did imagine it. He could just have slipped from there." "No, you weren't imagining things. I did that and yes, no one on this ship will believe you." Ananya said as she walked by him in the same direction.

"Where are you going?" He asked, but she didn't answer. Instead she looked at him through the corner of her eye and smiled. He followed her to the armory where she was greeted by the armory staff. Ananya began, "Sir, there were some issues with primary turret number four and secondary turrets number eight five and six three."

Andrew could not understand anything, but the armory master took the duo to the primary turret number four's base. The maintenance team was performing welding work on the gears and the servo motors. "The gears and the servo motors of the turret had been welded together and when it tried to move during the firing, it broke."

The trio went to the base of the other two turrets and found similar types of problems. The gears of one turret were re-arranged while the other had the cables cut-off. Ananya noted all the details and thanked him. "What were all those?" Andrew asked and she replied as they returned to the Captain's room. "Sabotage attempts."

The captain read the reports and sighed, "This is ridiculous. I don't know if I am supposed to deal with the enemies or this saboteur." Andrew knew about the seriousness of the issue and was also aware that the ship and the crew didn't take them particularly as allies, even if they don't consider them as enemies. "Have those repaired fast and prepare to move at maximum combat speed."

A few hours later, a strategic meeting was called and it was decided for the ship to resupply at Maldives. Maldives had an alignment towards China and even housed naval facilities for them. However, soon after the war began India captured the Island nation as it eliminated a serious threat of Chinese vessels in such close proximity.

After the topic had concluded, Ananya raised the issue of the sabotage attempts which have been increasing lately and advancing into combat sectors. The naval officers admitted the importance but were unable to find the culprit.

"Wait, you just said that lately the sabotage attempts have been advancing into the combat sector?" Andrew asked. "Yes, it's true. Damages to combat modules have increased in the past couple of days." Amaira replied. "Captain Amaira, may I know if you have any authority clearance system on the ship."

"Yes, we have and the clearances are updated regularly." Amaira responded to Andrew's question. Ananya popped another question, "What are authority clearances?" Naina replied, "In any warship, the captain defines who can visit which part of the vessel. The official term for this is authority clearance. Like by default, the bridge personnel can go anywhere, but the rest of the crew is not allowed to visit the bridge."

Ananya nodded and Andrew continued, "Who were the personnel given access to combat modules three days ago?" Amaira accessed the system to bring out six personnel who got access to combat modules. "Four of them are in the technical and maintenance teams. And the rest two are odd, captain why did you approve them?" Vivaan asked.

Amaira looked at their records, one was the quarter master while the other was his assistant. "The quarter master-? I don't recall upgrading his authority clearance." "So one of them or both of them could be..." Ananya began and the grown-ups nodded. They tried to think of a plan to get the saboteur but to no avail.

"Captain, I propose offering a bait to lure the real one out." The four officers already knew that Ananya and the saboteur are infiltrators. Amaira began, "So what's the plan?" "I'll be the bait. I am pretty sure, he won't resist such a bait." Ananya said with a sinister smile.

"What do you intent to do?" Andrew asked. Ananya explained the plan in detail leaving out the infiltrator part. "So do you agree on this?" Amaira asked and a grim silence followed. "This plan is too risky. I don't think we should place such a huge bet." Naina replied, surprising Ananya who remembered her not so friendly nature during her interrogation.

Vivaan and Arman too raised their concerns but agreed when Ananya's safety was guaranteed. Naina too agreed grudgingly and soon Ananya was housed in the brig while Andrew and his men guarded her. Chanakya's databanks were updated with the fact that Ananya had all information about the Chinese and their attack plans.

One of the Americans asked Andrew, "Is it true that she possessed the information about all Chinese plans and hid it from the captain?" Andrew had promised Ananya not to divulge her secret and replied, "Yes, it was the reason they fell prey to her firing. She fired in the direction where they'll move."

"So why is she here?" Max asked and he replied, "Serving a detention sentence for insubordination." Joe added, "And what are we doing here?" "After her little secret was open, Captain feared that she'll be targeted. She had to put it on official record, so there's a chance that people here might think her as a spy."

It was three in the afternoon of January 22, 2040. The quarter-master and his assistant arrived at her cell. They carried her meal and refreshments. One of Andrew's men stopped the duo, "Sorry, but we need to check everything." They checked the trays and the men to find no firearms of any sort of weapon.

"You are clear. Please proceed." He said after frisking the two of them. The duo went into the cell and kept the trays on the desk. "It's your food." The quarter master said and she responded, "Please keep it there and leave." "Sorry, but the captain ordered us to make sure you have the food." The other person responded.

Ananya sighed with discomfort and nodded. She got up from the bed and sat on the chair with the desk. "Um...Excuse me." She said and began eating. The two of them went to the cell door and waited for her to finish. As she finished her meal, the duo took the trays and left the cell.

The Americans watched the duo leave the area and just as they opened the door for them, a loud "THUDDD..." echoed in the hallway. "Catch them..." Andrew shouted as the nearest men jumped and grabbed the duo. Andrew and Max went inside the cell to find Ananya lying in a corner.

Four men brought the two men inside and Andrew checked Ananya for any life signs. "Max, inform the captain. She's no more." Max gritted his teeth and refrained from unbuckling the handgun from its holster, before going to the internal comm. link and telling the entire episode to the captain.

A few minutes later, Amaira entered the premise along with the naval officers. The duo was seated on chairs in front of them with the American guns trained on them. "So, these are the saboteurs." Amaira said as she looked at the lifeless Ananya in the corner.

Naina brought out her tab and said, "Quarter Master Gusphel Tsuring and Assistant Quarter Master Rittik Singh. Their records show nothing out of the ordinary." "So, you were here to get this ship captured right?" Rittik bellowed, "Huh...I won't be here for such a naïve cause. My mission was to infiltrate the mainland and weaken the society from inside."

Gusphel, the Quarter Master was completely silent. His face displayed a state of shock. "Why did you kill her?" Andrew asked and Rittik answered, "I didn't kill her. She was executed for killing thousands of Chinese nationals. She deserved that." He gave a sinister laughter that caused many of them want to kill him.

Amaira stopped the creaking triggers by a wave of her hand, "Tell me why I should not let these men kill you?" Giving off a smirk, he replied "You have every reason to kill both of us. We're also soldiers though unofficial." Vivaan moved forward, "What did you use to kill her?" "Her food was laced with Sodium Cyanide that we carry in order to commit suicide during capture. It was more than a lethal dose. She had no chance of surviving."

"Are you sure about that?" A voice came from the door. Everyone in the room was surprised and turned to see Ananya standing near the door, perfectly fine. Everyone was left jaw-dropped, even the four naval officers and Andrew who knew the whole plan were left surprised.

"Wait...How?" Andrew stammered unable to believe his eyes. "Lieutenant, you checked her correctly didn't you?" Joe asked and he replied, "Yes, I did. I didn't get her pulse at all." Ananya smiled and said, "He checked me all right. Even if someone were to check my pulse like that, they won't get any right now."

"So you didn't eat the food?" Rittik asked and she replied, "I ate that food and right now that cyanide must be reacting with the acid in my stomach." "But that should've killed you." "Where did you get that cyanide? China..." Ananya gave a little giggle.

Rittik immediately sprang to his feet and seized Naina's gun, holding her hostage at gunpoint. "You'll tell me how did you survive that cyanide?" Ananya reached out to her pocket and pulled out a half filled syringe. "Courtesy of this, you should've known that it's impossible to administer cyanide antidote without knowing the dose. So I took this anesthesia after experiencing first symptoms."

Ananya snatched the handgun of a nearby American and fired at Naina's leg. The bullet grazed past without any significant injuries but caused her to kneel and shout, "Are you mad?" The last word was muffled by the second gunshot that landed on Rittik's head.

"Why'd you kill him, he was the main culprit." Amaira shouted. "No, he wasn't the main culprit." Ananya said pointing the gun towards the shocked Gusphel. "Wait, he?" Vivaan asked. "The first lesson taught to any infiltrator – always keep a low profile. And always have a haughty and over-talkative sidekick."

Ananya pulled the trigger, aiming at the quarter master. He dodged the bullet at last moment and asked slowly, "How did the anesthesia save you?" Ananya re-aimed at him and replied, "It slowed down my metabolism by 70 to 80 percent. And so I am here." "You won't have much time, if it's that."

"Yeah, you're right. Taking into account the quality of cyanide, I still have an hour before any serious symptoms set in." Ananya replied as she supported her head with her hand. "Feeling dizzy?" He teased and Ananya fired in rapid succession.

Gusphel sprang into action, using the tray to guard against the bullets. As the last bullet was fired, he smashed the tray into the nearest soldiers. Ananya reloaded the gun and shot again in rapid succession. Gusphel threw the tray towards her and pulled up the desk to use as a shield.

Ananya dodged both the tray and the desk and threw the gun and the two magazines at his face. 'She is quite good in combat for a civilian.' Gusphel thought as he wrestled against Ananya, "You know too much about infiltrators, how so?" As the two struggled Amaira had the rest of men stand at a distance in order to keep them free of any flying objects.

He punched Ananya in the gut and pushed her away. She backed down, her body getting slow with every passing moment due to the anesthesia. "Now I see, you are an infiltrator as well." He shouted causing her to pause for a moment. The Americans were left in surprise as they whispered among themselves. "Oh, did I say something I shouldn't?" He giggled, "Now that your little secret is out, who'll be the main saboteur."

Ananya smirked and followed by a series of strikes. "They already know that." Gusphel's confidence vanished as he was rag dolled by Ananya. "Stop, please stop..." he begged, as Ananya held his combat knife at his throat. "Why now?" "We're both infiltrators, doesn't that make us comrades even if we're on the opposite sides."

"No...You and I both may be infiltrators, but there's a wide difference between us. You're officially trained, I am not. But still my training was far more rigorous and better than you had. One fact does not change is that you're a Chinese creation and you're bound to be defective. Mama's-boy!!!" She said as she pressed the knife closer and closer to his throat drawing out blood.

After a minute or so, she released the Chinese infiltrator and backed off, supporting her head with the bleeding arm. The Americans restrained the saboteur while Amaira helped Ananya and Vivaan and Arman helped Naina get to the infirmary. Barely after getting out of the cell, Ananya stopped moving and fell to the ground.

Amaira immediately kneeled to have a look at her, "It's bad, the effects have started." She said as she noticed her pale blue fingertips and the red patches over her face. She picked the girl up and rushed to the infirmary. Dr. Ram was already informed of the case and he kept all the preparations ready.

10

Ananya opened her eyes and looked at the roof for some time. 'Where am I? I am not on the ship.' She tried to push herself into sitting position and noticed the multiple catherers in her right arm. The door on her left opened and a doctor casually entered the room talking with someone behind.

The doctor concluded her talk and turned to see her struggle to get up. She rushed to the bed and helped her sit using support. "If I were you, I wouldn't try to push myself." He said. The doctor was a complete stranger and she asked, "Who are you? What is this place?" "Aah...You wouldn't know that. My name is Dr. Sanchi Ghosh and I am the surgeon who removed the remaining shrapnel from your body."

Ananya looked around to see three fluid bags hanging on an IV pole. "Where am I? And what are those?" Dr. Sanchi replied, "Today is January 24th, and you're in a naval hospital based in Maldives. Right now, you're being given glucose, blood fluid and sodium thiosulphate."

"Cyanide Poisoning!!!" She sighed and removed the blanket covering her, trying to stand. "No, don't even try to stand now." She said, pushing her legs back into the blanket, "Don't even try to stand before the therapy is complete. Your body withstood extreme strain and according to what Dr. Ram told me, you deserve a rest."

"I had a two day rest and moreover, the ship needs me." She said as the doctor elevated the bed to allow her to recline and rest. "You took an excessive dose of cyanide. It would be better if the therapy is completed before you go."

Ananya looked at the side-table to see a bouquet of flowers in a vase. "Those flowers are beautiful, what are those?" "The yellow ones are Beach Hibiscus and the pink ones are Frangipani. These flowers are exotic to Maldives." She looked around as the doctor added two syringes of a fluid into the glucose bag. Dr. Sanchi smiled, "Don't be all that suspicious. That's just adrenaline, it'll help speed up the recovery process."

"No, it's not that. Do you know who brought those flowers?" Ananya asked. "Oh, you weren't awake at that time. Well they're a gift from your captain." "Captain..." "Yeah, she visits you every six hours since the ship got into the port." Ananya was surprised at the information and laid silently for about another half hour before Dr. Sanchi let her out of the bed.

She was discharged after being declared fit enough to not need constant care and her discharge documents were handed over to Dr. Ram. "Captain, Weapons Control Officer Ananya Anand reporting back on duty." She saluted Amaira as they met on the bridge. "I see you're in good health. Well let's see what your reports say."

Dr. Ram, who came with Ananya said, "You should probably not see that." "Why so?" Amaira responded and went through the reports. "You got to be kidding." She shrieked as she read half of the report. "Nah, it's true. That's why he told you not to read it." Ananya smiled as she got glares from Amaira and the doctor.

"Bruises on bones, twenty total stitches for shrapnel removal, high blood toxicity levels and double bone density. Is there anything left?" Amaira sighed, slamming her forehead into her palm. "I don't think, I'll stay alive for long with all this. That's for sure..." She added making Ananya giggle a little.

She was reading the report of Ananya's final full body check-up, after which she was discharged. She handed over the report to Dr. Ram and asked, "How was she declared fit to be discharged?" "Well she's not completely fit but rather fit enough that she doesn't need constant care."

Ananya took her station and since they were in a port, there was nothing much that she could do. "Umm...Captain, what happened to Commander Naina? I wanted to apologize for shooting her in the heat of the moment?" "I am very fine, thank you. I would have preferred that apology directly, Weapons Control Officer." Naina replied as she entered the room.

It was quite early in the morning and having nothing to do, bored her quickly. She came out on the deck and began to walk around. She could see many people working with the ship all over. "What happened? I don't remember this much damage to be caused during any skirmish."

"Well you can blame the A.I. Assistant for this." Vivaan said as he emerged behind her with Andrew. "Lt. Andrew was manning your station while you were unconscious." Ananya gave a smile and asked, "What are your observations?" Andrew gulped and looked here and there. "What are you talking about?" He laughed off nervously.

"I'm an infiltrator. I am more adept in your job than you, so don't lie. Since the first mission, you were trying to get to the weapon control station. So, how was it?" Andrew was left at a loss of words and he admitted, "Well, it was hell tough to control where the gun's moving. It never locked on the target; I had to fire all shots with guesses."

Ananya turned towards the railing and bent to look at the work before straightening up uncomfortably. "Well, looks like your experience saved the ship. I hope you didn't use suppressive fire mode and kept it at single shot." Andrew scratched his head, trying to figure the meaning of the little girl's words.

"Well, I think you do owe an explanation on yourself." Andrew smirked and she replied, "You heard that twice, I am an infiltrator." "You mean a spy?" Andrew asked and Vivaan replied, "No, more like a mix of a soldier and a spy. Her combat training is superior to a normal spy while her espionage training is superior to that of a soldier."

"I don't think why would you need them? This work can be easily done by highly trained spies of CIA." This comment from Andrew caused Ananya to laugh out of control. "What's there to laugh?" Vivaan asked and she replied, "Why shouldn't I laugh? My training missions were to subdue or eliminate spies in Vishakhapatnam, back when it was the naval HQ. And I got at least twelve CIA agents among the fifty targets."

The trio was having the conversation when the Harbor Master hurriedly went to the bridge. They noticed him and followed him. As soon as he reported the matter to Amaira, the trio entered to find her worried about some matter. "We need to convene an emergency meeting. Meet in the strategy room in 240."

Her tone seemed grim and the trio nodded. In five minutes, the six of them met in the strategy room. Amaira explained the situation to them, "Maldives is being blockaded by the Chinese forces. Their navy from Africa is on the west and the Hambantota forces in the east. There are in total thirty vessels, and according to the harbor master they are small and fast ships. Three cruisers, seven destroyers, eight corvettes, six frigates and six patrol vessels."

Naina and Vivaan noted, "We can't push through this swarm by brute strength. We'll have to use some other tactic." "How much time do we have before the repairs are finished?" Ananya asked. Amaira answered, "Please refrain from asking irrelevant questions during a strategic meet."

"No, I do mean it. Please tell me?" Ananya insisted and Andrew grumbled, "Just tell her, you're wasting more time." "Our repairs will be finished in four hours. So, what of it?" Naina replied. But instead of answering her question, Ananya asked another question "Which one is their flag-ship?"

Amaira brought out a map and pointed to a ship in the South-West direction. "This cruiser has done least movement according to our spotters. Most probably, this is the flagship. But what'll you do with this information." Ananya smiled and said, "Keep the schedule as planned. I'll create an opening near the flagship in exactly 4 hours 30 minutes from now."

Everyone was surprised and Vivaan asked, "What are you going to do?" "Something that I was trained to do." She answered cryptically. "I disapprove." Amaira spoke and the three naval officers agreed with her. Naina began, "Weapons Control Officer, since you're the only one here capable of utilizing our limited resources. We're not allowing you to go on any rampaging solo missions."

Vivaan added, "You can tell us your plan." Ananya sighed and nodded, "My plan is to infiltrate the flagship and sabotage their formation near it. At that time, our ship will move out from there and I'll rendezvous with the ship here about two nautical miles north from here."

The plan was good but knowing how her previous plans went, the naval officers were not willing to risk their most precious resource on this mission. But again, only she was trained as a professional infiltrator who could do such a feat. The five grown-ups went to a corner and discussed the matter.

"All right, your plan is approved. But to ensure that you don't do anything crazy, I and Lieutenant Andrew will accompany you." Amaira said. Though Ananya wanted to oppose the idea, she had to agree reluctantly. "I think I'll leave it to you grown-ups to find a good background." The five of them thought while Ananya took leave to bring some items.

She returned in fifteen minutes with a big school bag. "What's in that?" "Some things that'll help us in the mission. Do you know any explosive expert? One who can make those undetectable?" She replied to Andrew who thought for a while and replied, "Maybe Donald can. But why?"

"We'll need them. Usually I make them personally, but we're running low on time." She replied while searching for something in her bag. She looked again at Andrew, "Do you have your passport?" "What?" "Do you have your passport or any civilian ID?"

"Yes, I carry my passport in my personal belongings." Andrew put his hand inside his uniform to bring out a wet American Passport. Ananya however didn't even look at the passport and said, "Yes, that'll do." She pulled out two small handbags from her bag. They had letters 'T' and 'M' written with permanent markers.

She opened the 'T' marked handbag and turned it upside down. Out came multiple passports of different countries. There were more than hundred passports. Naina shrieked, "What are these?" "Identifications used by my targets. Let's see we have these..." Ananya replied as she searched the pile for American passports. "...All right, I have these ten female American passports. Captain, take anyone you like."

She put back all the passports in the handbag and opened the next handbag. But instead of flipping it over, she pulled out a single American passport. "This one's mine." Arman snooped over to look at the bag and was shocked to see the same number of passports there. "Whoa, whose passports are those?" He exclaimed and Ananya responded in an uncomfortable tone, "Mine."

Amaira chose her passport, one belonging to someone called, 'Hillary Rogers'. "Okay, please remember that name." Ananya said as she put the rest nine passports in the handbag. Ananya next pulled out two leather bands with many spring contraptions. She bent to pull out two combat knives from her dress.

Another four combat knives were pulled out of the bag and fitted in the spring contraptions. Two small bars were also added. Everyone watched silently as she prepared the contraption and went out, "Captain, you should change into some civilian clothing."

The trio met again about half hour later in the same room, everyone wore civilian dresses and weren't looking like soldiers in any sense. "Here take these." Ananya said handing over a pile of notes to Amaira. "These are US Dollars, but why are they so hot." "Oh, they just came out of the printer." Ananya responded pointing to the printer behind her back. It spat out another sheet containing the front prints of American notes.

"You're forging identity, currency and documents. Don't you think it'll be too dangerous? CIA agents spend months to build up the identity." Andrew began and Ananya smiled, "We'll be back on the ship before they could even verify our documents." She cut the paper into note sizes and glued them on a plastic sheet.

Donald arrived in the room with a small bag and handed it over to Andrew. "Okay kid, here's your C4. Now?" Ananya responded, "We'll have to carry them." She pulled out a couple of explosive devices and put them inside her handbag. Amaira and Andrew followed suit and hid more than twenty explosive devices.

"That should be good. Did you think of a background story?" Ananya said. "How about this one? We're adventurers from the US and our boat got screwed. This'll grant us ample time to conduct the mission and escape." Andrew began and got a response immediately, "Rejected!!!"

Amaira brought up the next idea, "We were on a cruise ship that got sunk accidently and we're running low on supplies. I think this will lessen their scrutiny on us." The entire room was engulfed with silence until Ananya finally spoke, "Is there a recent shipwreck nearby?" Naina pointed at the map a little north from there. "Here is a cruise liner that was sunk yesterday. The reason's not clear but most suggest it a pirate incident."

"Do you think they'll believe it?" Ananya asked and Naina nodded, "I can't say. But on that shouldn't you know that better?" Ananya sighed, "It's too quick to think about. But personally I could've caused a whole shipwreck just to get in." The statement left a grim atmosphere until she added another statement, "Just kidding."

"Okay. It's all set up for now. The only thing remains is to wait." "Why wait? You should strike right now." Vivaan suggested. "Patience is always a virtue." Ananya said as she looked at the map closely. "We'll need a boat, preferably a small and speedy one."

Ananya tampered with Amaira's passport to fit her photo. As she was done with it, she handed it over to Amaira, "Captain, remember that name." Amaira nodded and asked, "What's your name?" Ananya opened her passport and flipped it over, "I'll go by the name Emma Dale. We don't know each other before the shipwreck and only befriended to survive."

About an hour later, Ananya finished the documentation and stretched only to wither in pain and return back to prior position. "Background is ready and now..." She stood up and moved towards the door. "Where are you going?" Naina asked and Ananya raised her right hand, showing the cannula inserted in her hand.

"You seriously want this to be removed?" Dr. Ram explained as Ananya and Amaira asked him to temporarily remove the cannula. "Yes doctor, she is going on an undercover mission. Please you've to do this." Dr. Ram sighed, "Okay." And he proceeded with the process. Most of her arm's bandages were also removed, exposing the multiple stitches she had.

At three o'clock, the repair and resupply was completed and the trio took the boat departing from the port. "Keep the ship ready to move out at level one battlestations." Amaira gave all instructions to Naina who'll be the acting captain. Ananya reluctantly handed her station to Joe, who according to Andrew was good in handling weaponry. "The system automatically locks the targets. You'll only have to fire, don't mess with the target lock."

11

It was 3:10 and on the Chinese Type 178 light cruiser, Ensign Lee Chen Chang was on spotting duty when he spotted three people being washed towards them by the waves. He immediately informed the commanding officer in Chinese, "We have some unidentified people being washed up towards us."

The officer immediately responds, "Are they alive or dead?" The spotter responded, "Unsure. They aren't showing any specific movements. Maybe a dead man's float." The commanding officer orders the deck crew to pull the trio onboard.

The deck crew fished out the trio, who seemed to be floating for quite some time. They were taken to a room and provided blankets to warm them. The trio consisted of a man, a woman and a teen. Ensign Lee was assigned to keep an eye on them and try to get as much information as possible.

As they normalized, the Ensign informed the seniors of the update. "Are you feeling well?" He asked in the translator device hooked in his uniform. The trio nodded in affirmative. "Which country are you from? Are you Indians?" He asked again and one by one the three of them replied, "I am Andrew Gibbs. American!" "I am Hillary Rogers. American!" Only the teenager was left, his eyes trained on her as she answered, "I am Emma Dale. Again American."

He however didn't state that their answers were being recorded and heard by his seniors. "So, how did you end up in the sea?" Emma spoke up, "We were on the Saint Atlantis cruise liner. Maybe yesterday or day before yesterday, the liner sunk and since then we were on the mercy of the waves."

The senior officers took notes from their conversations, "There was a shipwreck report in the last information update." The Ensign asked, "Can I see your boarding passes or tickets." Hillary answered, "It was total chaos and I only managed to grab my passport before jumping out of the window."

She took out an almost wet passport from her handbag. He took the passport and opened it, "Hillary Rogers." He looked at the remaining two who brought out their passports. "Do you guys know each other?" Andrew responded with a grim voice, "No, not before the shipwreck."

Lee went out of the room and talked with the superior officers. Since the satellite passed over just an hour ago, they'll have to wait for at least five hours before they could verify the information. He went to the room and saw the trio in a slightly better situation. "Sorry but it looks like verifying your information will take some time. Till that time feel comfortable here."

"Why is this ship here?" Emma asked in Chinese getting a surprised look by the trio. Since the superior officers weren't on the other side, convincing them of this fact would be near impossible. "You know Chinese?" He asked surprisingly, turning off his translator. "Yes, I've learnt Chinese in the school. But you didn't tell me, why are you here?"

Unable to determine the next course of action, he simply told her, "This is a Chinese cruiser and we're blockading Maldives to stop and capture a rogue battleship." Emma nodded in understanding and asked again, "Aren't you too young to be a soldier?" This time however, she asked in English showing that her proficiency in Chinese wasn't that much high.

"No, I am 19 and perfectly eligible to give duties in the People's Liberation Army." He answered in Chinese and hoped that she didn't understand most of it. He left the room and went to his senior officer. As he entered the cabin of the commanding officer, he saw some officers preparing to leave. He went to the officer and saluted him.

"Ensign Lee, is there anything strange from our guests?" The officer asked and he replied, "The teen knows Chinese, a little bit."

"Hmm...What's their nature? Anything suspicious?" "No, they are not too much friendly and I do think they suspect us of something. I don't think they believed in anything we said." Lee responded.

The officer laughed it off and lit a cigar, "It's nothing. Well it does add to the legitimacy that they might be civilians from the shipwreck. Once we confirm that, I'll have them sent to Mainland and then to the American embassy. They can probably take care of the rest." "Sir, my orders?" The officer stretched on the seat and replied, "Try to be friendly with them. You know when they get back to America, we'll be projected as heroes. And that will help us to get their support against those barbaric Indians."

"Sir, aren't you too much confident that they are genuine Americans. What if they're spies?" The officer smiled again bringing out the three passports and a piece of paper. "Son, this paper contains the list of people who are missing in the Saint Atlantis case. And here look who we have on number 314, 516 and 879." Lee looked at the paper and saw the names at the corresponding numbers.

314, Andrew Gibbs, American, 37

516, Hillary Rogers, American, 30

879, Emma Dale, American, 15

"I see, so why don't you send them right now dad?" Lee asked. And the officer, his dad replied, "Actually this is an unofficial list released by the CNN and BBC. We got this in the last update from the SAT-LINK. I'll just send this for verification in Mainland."

Lee left the room to check on the new guests, turning on his translator. "Sorry to see you waiting." He entered the room to the see the trio sitting as is. "Well, if you aren't feeling comfortable here, you can go on the deck as well. It's quite sunny there." The trio agreed and he took them to the deck where they stayed till the trio got dried up.

"I don't want to be personal, but what do you do back in your country." Lee asked and the trio answered one by one. "Well, I was a senator until the last election." Andrew replied. Hillary added, "I worked as a freelance news reporter." Emma finally stated, "I am just a high-school student."

Lee smiled at her answer, causing her to draw sharp reaction "What about to laugh?" Lee immediately switched to apologetic mode, "I didn't mean to be rude, but the way you said it just...Like, you're so lucky growing up in a country far away from any war or turmoil. I wish I could've said the same thing to someone so easily."

Andrew smiled and added with sympathy, "I knew a military man who died few days back, he used to say that children are worst affected in a war. Now I see why he used to say so." "If you don't mind, I'll love to see your warship from inside. I mean if it doesn't hinder your work."

Lee thought for a while on Hillary's request. She was media personnel, so showing her the warship was a bad idea. But it could serve well as propaganda as well. He wished to ask the commanding officer on this, but he was busy trying to figure out a plan to capture the Indian Battleship. He approached Hillary and responded, "Okay, I'll only show you the ship's non strategic parts."

They nodded and he led them through the narrow hallway of the ship's interior to show the Engine room, the plotting room, the living quarters, the diner and the spotting tower. He escorted them back to their room and stood on guard outside it.

• • • •

"WHAT TO DO NOW ANANYA? As you asked I asked him to show us parts of the ship. Did you get what you needed?" Amaira asked in a hushed voice. Ananya sighed, "Captain, we'll have to get into the armory first." "So genius, you got some idea?" Andrew asked which resulted in Ananya giving him a malicious smile.

She went to the door and knocked. Lee entered the room and she asked, "Actually, could you please provide us some food?" Lee smiled and nodded. He went out towards the diner, leaving the door open. The trio quickly scrambled and went out. "This is a Chinese Type 178 light cruiser. The armory we need to go must be one level below the deck, right on the centerline." Ananya explained as they ran through the relatively unguarded hallway.

They entered the supposed room and quickly locked it from inside. "Is this the armory? I don't see any armaments." Andrew taunted grimly at the almost empty room. Ananya looked around and found a small board with text in Chinese. "Torpedo Feeder." She read. "We are at the correct spot, just one level higher." Amaira added.

Soon, the crew realized that their guests have gone missing. "We can't go outside now. We'll have to go right through the floor." Ananya said as she opened her hand bag and brought out clay like substance. "You're simply crazy. Man, where am I struck." Andrew sighed as she applied a uniform thickness circle of the clay and stepped back.

She pulled out a small battery and two wires putting the wires into the clay. "Here goes, three, two, one and..." She connected the battery at one and then there was a sound of a muffled explosion. The area covered with the clay vanished and she said, "Let's go to the armory." The two ladies vanished into the hole, leaving behind an awe-filled and surprised Andrew.

Andrew jumped at last only to find him and the duo hiding from the Chinese crew who were in the room. "There are cameras all around." Andrew said as he saw three cameras looking around. Ananya quickly went around the nearest Chinese personnel and just as he spotted the duo and shouted, "What are you..." His throat was slashed by Ananya from behind.

Two knives with slightly curved blades appeared in her hands as she quickly leapt on the remaining two personnel killing them off swiftly. "When did you get those?" Andrew shouted while Amaira quickly normalized and took the handgun of slain personnel to shoot down the cameras.

"They must've noticed by now that we're not civilians. We must hurry. Captain, that's the starboard wall." She pointed to the wall in front of her. "Rig it with the explosives and Lieutenant Andrew, you have the port wall over there." She went to the huge columns of torpedoes and began to arm them, one stack at a time.

The trio finished their work in ten minutes and realized that Chinese soldiers have gathered outside the door, banging it and shouting – 'Come out with your hands in the air. Surrender now and you won't be harmed.' "Even if we have done our job here, we must return alive. What to do next?" Amaira asked and Ananya winked, "We'll surrender."

Andrew opened the door and the trio came out, their hands in the air. "Hope you have a way around." Andrew whispered in Ananya's ear. "Put you weapons down." The crew member shouted and Amaira put down her gun on the floor before returning to the former position. Andrew too followed suit.

All guns trained on Ananya who held a switch in her right hand. "Put that thing down and do the same as your comrades did." Little did they know that the switch was already pressed. Ananya bent down and put the switch on the ground. "Now straighten up and put your hand behind your head." He shouted again pointing the assault rifle towards her.

"You'll be sorry, if I release this." Ananya said, her face having a strange smile. "I said, straighten up!!!" The crew member shouted shooting a bullet near her leg. She slowly left the switch and straightened slowly. "Ten...Nine...Eight..." She began counting and continued.

"...Seven...Six...Five...Four..." "Hey, what are you counting?" Another crew member shouted as he heard her during the frisking. "...Three...Two...One..." "SHUT UP!!!!" He hit the butt of the gun on her face and she counted. "ZERO!!!"

Multiple sailors began to scream and fell to the ground, as if they were electrocuted. "Ready...SET...GO!!!" She screamed as she punched the two crewmen in the chest. The two men leaned over her arms as a 'KLAANG' sound came from her hands.

She withdrew her hand and drew out the six combat knives that stabbed the two men. Before the rest of them could gain composure, the three of them made quick work of them. "Hurry, we're going neck-to-neck with the schedule. To the bridge!!!" The trio hurried to the bridge, making way through dead sailors.

"What happened to them?" Amaira asked and she replied, "They took all our fake currencies. Rest I'll explain on the ship." They reached the bridge to find four high ranking officers all right. "They didn't take the notes." Ananya clicked her tongue. 'This will delay us.'

Before the elders could make a move, she immediately threw the six combat knives towards the Chinese and equipped the two curved knives to charge on the senior-most officers. Surprised by the sudden reckless charge, the two backed-off causing her to slash their uniform instead of throat.

"Don't move!!!" Four guns trained at Ananya while Amaira and Andrew put theirs on the officers. "You'd better put yours down; we're having this ship hostage." Andrew shouted. 'Three Indian spies are having this entire ship, the flagship of the blockade hostage. They killed most of the crew without even...' The fleet head's chain of thought was broken when a high caliber bullet brushed past his nose.

Immediately realizing his weak position in front of the enemies, he lowered his gun and said "Can't we talk it out?" The Chinese officers followed suit and lowered their guns. "I am Rear Admiral Lui Klang. It's good to meet some skilled players of this game." "So war is a game for you." Amaira asked and he replied, "Yes, like a fine game of chess."

Ananya withdrew her curved knives and pulled back the six knives. "They're connected by a thread, Impressive!!!" Lui added. "May I know your names?" The four officers were clustered near the windshield with Amaira and Andrew training their weapons on them.

Amaira gave a look to Ananya who meddled with the controls of the bridge and gave a nod. "I never thought you guys took orders from a teen." Lui smirked "Field experience matters the most to us." Andrew responded and Lui continued, "I still want to know the names of the skilled players, starting with you gentleman."

Amaira whispered in Andrew's ear as he began, "My name is Andrew Gibbs. Lieutenant Commander of the United States' Third Scout Fleet." His introduction left a bad taste on the Chinese and one of them said something in Chinese only to be translated immediately by Ananya. "I never thought that US would betray our Seoul deal."

"Man, you know Chinese that well?" Lui asked. "The first step to know your enemy is to know their past, culture and language." She replied as she went from one battlestation to other. "My name is Amaira Gupta. Captain of your target ship INS Chanakya."

The eight Chinese eyes turned towards Ananya who paused for a while to introduce herself briefly, "My name is Ananya Anand." "Aren't you with them?" Lui asked only to get no reaction from any of them. "You're the one who's doing all the talking. Who're they?" Amaira asked pointing her gun towards the other three.

The trio introduced them one-by-one, "I am Lieutenant Commander Xiaou Feng." "I am Commander Mi Xiaping." "I am the Captain, my name is Dong Chen Chang." Just as the Captain introduced himself, a man entered the bridge and charged on Amaira.

Andrew saw it by the corner of his eye and immediately pushed her aside. The man tackled Andrew with all his might and wrestled with him for his gun. The four officers sprang into action and seized their weapons from Amaira and Andrew. "You, move away from the battlestations kid."

Ananya obliged and stood with Amaira and Andrew as Mi checked the status and exclaimed. "All torpedoes have been programmed to attack our allied ships." "Reprogram them..." Lui shouted but she replied, "It isn't possible without the access keys." Lui and Dong searched their uniforms to find the keys missing.

"Where are the keys?" He shouted as Mi and Xiaou began to search around for them. "Hey, looking for these?" Ananya asked as she showed a single key. The slashes on the officers were initially meant to get the access keys, which they hung in a locket. The two officers looked in horror as she had combined them to make the master key, giving her access to all functions of the ship.

"Put the ship on lockdown. Override all administrative access." Lui ordered. Mi protested, "If we do that, this ship will be only a floating bulls-eye. We cant..." Lui interrupted her, "If she's smart enough to take the access keys and create the master key. She can use this ship against our allies."

Mi reluctantly agreed and put the entire ship on lockdown. "Do it." Ananya said slowly as the lockdown message played through the entire ship. "Aah..." Mi cried before she fell on the ground, blood pouring out of her head. Xiaou shouted, "What the..." but couldn't complete as he was shot immediately by Amaira.

Andrew kicked the man and knocked him to the wall. "It's you. Ensign Lee, our guide." Lee immediately stood up, tears in his eyes "I won't let you Indians take control our..." He gave a loud wail of cry as Ananya threw one of her knives towards him and pulled it back at the last moment.

"Were you saying something? Captain! ask Commander to begin." She said in a grim tone as he collapsed on the floor, tears flowing like rivers from his eyes. "I was..." Lui kicked Ananya, knocking off the knives along with their threads before slamming her through the bullet-proof windshield. The glass shattered on impact with many shards piercing her.

Lui too came out of the window, drawing out his handgun in the process. Ananya ducked and rolled to avoid the bullets, exaggerating the wounds by the glass shards. She quickly grabbed a maintenance rod on the deck and knocked the gun off Lui's hand as he was reloading.

The two of them fought toe-to-toe, as Lui managed to even the field by taking advantage of the long lance-like movements of the rod. Lui suddenly grabbed the rod by its pointed end and smirked, "You're too good of a fighter for being Indian. I always thought Indians were born pacifists, to think someone from that country would have such prowess and intellect. But alas, we were the better civilization at every point of time."

Ananya smiled with malice, "You and better? Huh, I saw that when you ordered the ship on lockdown. What did you say; if she is smart enough to create the master key she can use our ship to attack our allies. You didn't think, if I am smart enough to arm and program your armaments right in front of you I must have thought of a backup."

She brought out the master key and threw it in the sea. Lui turned away in the direction of throw and she used the moment to close up the distance and brought out her remaining knife and stabbed him in the chest. Lui grabbed the knife and slumped there. "Over-confident fool." She cursed him and took the binoculars to see that the Chanakya has begun to move out of the port.

She pulled out another remote trigger device and was about to press the button when, "Don't do that. That is if you want to see your comrades alive." Dong said as he and Lee emerged from the opposite side of the ship. Two guns were in his hands with Amaira and Andrew walking just in front of them.

"What happened?" She asked and Dong replied, "Your lovely captain left her gun unattended when she was contacting your ship." Ananya gave a strange expression as if asking Amaira, 'Seriously?' Amaira seemed to understand the infiltrator's look and nodded. Ananya sighed, almost feeling like it's a joke.

"Now, hand over that little thing. Whatever it is." Lui said, suddenly jumping and pointing another gun towards Ananya. "There's no use little girl. No matter how much trained fighter you are, you could never have guessed that a navy officer would be having a steel plate inside his uniform." He pulled out the plate from beneath his neck and showed the dent her knife made on it.

He released the safety of the gun and repeated, "Give me that thing." Ananya smiled and said, "With pleasure." She pushed the button and flung the trigger towards the Admiral. Within seconds, multiple explosions rocked the ship. Lee came to the windshield and shouted, "We've got multiple explosions both on port and starboard side. Compartments are flooding at levels one through four."

"Damn you!!!" Lui shouted as he shot Ananya, who darted out of the way but still was hit in the chest, right towards the heart. She collapsed towards the railing, blood dripping from the wound. Soon her body grew lifeless and stopped any kind of activity. Tears flowed from Andrew and Amaira's eyes as they saw a teen becoming victim of the war, adults started.

"It's no use, cursing yourself won't do anything. Captain. The best way to honor her sacrifice would be to win this war." Andrew said to Amaira, who nodded and wiped her tears. "Awww...Looks like you two are too close to her. Why don't we send you to hell with her? You can play wargames there." Dong said.

"Captain, allow me to have the honor." Lui asked as he trained the guns towards them. "I won't let you two die that easily." He shot Amaira in her right arm and asked, "I want a detailed design report of your ship. I know I can't capture it now that this ship is practically junk but that will ensure my promotion to Vice Admiral." Andrew tried to move in defiance but couldn't as Dong had guns trained on both Andrew and Amaira.

Amaira's arm began to bleed heavily and she knew why. 'The wound has been re-opened. It took a full week to stop bleeding from there.' She thought as the pain intensified. Lui again shot her, this time the bullet went grazing past her knee and she slumped down. Lui moved forward towards her, "Tell me, or else this pain will increase exponentially."

Amaira suddenly felt relaxed, she knew her life was flowing out as blood and soon she'll die. But she couldn't help but feel the comfort. As her strength drained with the blood, all the struggles seized to exist and she smiled. 'My part is over.' She smiled and with tear filled eyes pointed her index finger on her forehead.

Everyone was surprised by the action. "She is asking me to kill her but I won't. Listen, you won't die unless you tell me about that ship." Lui pulled her hair and shouted in her ear but it hardly affected her. Andrew flew into a fit of rage and attacked Dong knocking the guns from his hands. Lui trained his gun again towards Amaira as Andrew and Dong brawled.

"Maybe I should end your suffering." Lui muttered as he applied pressure on the trigger looking at the semi-conscious Amaira. "No you won't." A voice came from his right. He unconsciously turned to his right to find Ananya standing right next to him. Her bloodied hands carried the same pointed rod which she spun thrice before stabbing Lui with the pointed end.

The surprise caused him to pull the trigger, but sudden motion caused the bullet to miss her heart and went grazing by her belly. Amaira fell unconscious as the rod went right through Lui and Ananya said, "No amount of steel can protect you against this." She pushed the rod further and further until the rod and Lui hit the ship's wall.

"HOW!?" Lui asked and Ananya brought out a similar metal plate from underneath her dress. "Oversmart!!!" Though the bullet didn't kill her, it did pierce the steel plate and hit her. "Lieutenant, take care of captain." She shouted while the retrieval mechanism of her arm bands, which were very much visible then; pulled the combat knives back.

Andrew disengaged with Dong and tended Amaira's wounds. Applying pressure through the wounds and tying tourniquets near them, he managed to stop the bleeding. Meanwhile, Ananya overpowered Dong and held him with knife at throat. "DAAAAD...!!!" Lee's voice echoed and they saw him standing behind the remaining bulletproof windshield.

Ananya ordered him to come out by gesture and waited till he stood in front of her. "Do you love your father?" She asked and he nodded in affirmative. "Do you love him more than yourself?" Ananya asked again and Lee nodded after thinking for a while. She hit a nearby gun by her shoe and ordered him, "Pick it up."

Lee resisted only for Ananya to bring her knife closer to Dong's throat, "Do it!!!" Lee hurriedly bent down and picked the gun up. "Now, Shoot!!!" She shouted. Lee screamed and almost dropped the gun in fear. "Shoot, or else he'll die." She brought the knife closer, drawing out blood.

Lee screamed again and shot, his aim went haywire and missed the duo by a mile. Ananya smiled with malice, "Good!!!" and rushed towards him and hit him with her combat knife in the shoulder. She didn't hit him hard, only a pinch but he gave a loud wail and fell unconscious. Ananya sighed in disappointment and took out the next remote trigger.

Dong crawled to his son, tears flowing from his eyes. "What did you do to him?" He asked Ananya who answered, "Simply shown him the difference between your propaganda videos and actual combat. The difference between fantasies and reality. When he wakes up, that is if he ever does, he'll be a different person."

Andrew in the meantime managed to bring Amaira back into consciousness. The trio looked at the approaching Chanakya and Ananya said, "It's time for round two." And pressed the trigger. The explosives set by Amaira and Andrew blew up one by one.

The explosions resulted in destruction of the walls that separated the flooded compartments and the torpedo armory. The programmed and armed torpedoes' propellers sprung into action as soon as they touched the water and sped towards their targets.

Six ships on both sides, i.e. starboard and port w.r.t. the flagship were sunk in the following five minutes making more than enough space for the Chanakya to speed away. All other blockading ships received multiple submarine alerts from the flagship which caused them to disengage immediately.

12

Camorta, Andaman and Nicobar Islands

"The entire blockading fleet disengaged. On whose orders." Admiral Wang asked the officer who brought him the report. "Admiral, all ships received multiple submarine alerts and just after that the flagship and the nearby ships were sunk by torpedoes. The next in-command ordered a withdrawal." The officer replied.

"They're getting closer to Porbander and we don't have anything on them." He gestured the officer to leave and pondered upon the strategy. "This one ship is causing me so much trouble. I..." He picked the paperweight and threw it against a wall in frustration.

A knock came on the door and Wang said, "COME IN!!!" after adjusting his uniform. Another officer came in with a slim tab. "Sir, I have design comparison of all second world war battleships of US and Germany." "Finally, a good news. Show me."

He placed the tab on the table and showed him many black and white pictures. "These are German battleships. They were exceptionally notorious for their survivability and accuracy." He zoomed on a ship, "This is the Bismarck, perhaps the most famous of all. His armor scheme was notorious for the all round protection. It had four main turrets each housing two guns."

Wang added, "If I am correct, this ship one shot HMS Hood." "Yes sir, it's true. It was perhaps the shortest battleship-to-battleship fight." "Weakness." "Bismarck had relatively weak armor protection on its guns and stern. Other than that I know nothing, it is said to stay afloat after suffering 2600 AP shells at point blank and more than 100 torpedoes."

Wang nodded and ordered, "Next?" "Sir, this is Bismarck's sister ship Tirpitz. It was the peak of German shipbuilding industries progress. It featured reinforced turret and deck armor and survived air raids for about two years before being sunk by a magazine explosion caused by an earthquake bomb." "Earthquake bomb?" "Sir these bombs were specially designed to destroy buried air-raid bunkers. They were reported to destroy bunkers upto 100 meters deep."

"Superior AA?" "Yes sir, according to some unofficial sources this ship had the most effective AA." Wang again nodded and asked, "What's next?" "Sir this one's a bit interesting. It's the only battleship known to be equipped with torpedo launchers. Its name is Gneisenau." "Where were they equipped?" "They were equipped under the deck with openings under rear turrets."

"That explains the torpedoes and AA. What about missiles? Is there any battleship..." "Yes sir. This is the USS Iowa class battleship. During their re-armament in the 1980s, they were equipped with missile launchers capable of launching Tomahawk missiles." "Any special mentions?"

"Sir, I went actually a little out of the way to figure out their defenses like the torpedo problems etc." "So what are the results?" The officer now showed the photo of a submarine, "Sir this is a German submarine or U-boat. U-2679 as it was called; it was designed in such a way that only torpedoes hitting the top part would cause any damage. Hit it at any other angle and they'll ricochet like shells."

"So, what you're saying is that the ship may be build keeping that design in mind?" "Yes sir, it's completely possible. And since ships have very less underwater surface portion, maybe that ship is completely invulnerable to torpedoes." Wang's face washed away in surprise, "So they created a ship completely immune to the ship killers."

"Sir, I do have a plan that could possibly defeat the ship before it goes into the naval stronghold. It's very risky although." "Go on. It's more risky to let that ship go into naval stronghold. I'll manage the higher ups." The officer told the plan to Wang in extreme detail trying to predict what decisions the ship's captain would take.

After going through the plan, Wang admitted, "This is risky but worth a shot. And I'll have it broadcasted live across the world. Just think of the headline 'INDIAN NAVY LEFT BEHIND A FELLOW SHIP TO ESCAPE THE CHINESE NAVAL MIGHT: SAILORS AT CHINESE MERCY'. It'll be great for propaganda. Tell the communications officer to contact our men in all international media platforms and transmit them the data I'll forward him."

Wang wrote down three notes and gave them to the officer who took them ad left. The notes were addressed to Gwadar Outpost, Hambantota Outpost and International Media Agents. "Its time for the Endgame." He called another officer and asked him to prepare a ship that'll go back to mainland.

• • • •

Infirmary of INS Chanakya

AMAIRA OPENED HER EYES in the infirmary and looked around. "I see you're finally awake captain." Dr. Ram said as he checked her up and helped her to sitting position. "What happened?" She asked as she looked at her right arm restrained in a splinter. "You had three bullet wounds and a lot of blood loss."

She looked at the next bed to find Ananya lying there, unconscious. Dr. Ram followed her gaze and said, "She was in a worse condition. A bullet hit on the chest, back filled with glass shards, blunt weapon hit on face and what not. Like she already was in any good condition."

Amaira remembered as Ananya triggered the second round of explosions; the ship they were on began to capsize. The three of them jumped into the sea as soon as possible and tried to swim away. The salt water hurt in her wounds and increased the blood loss. They swam for two minutes before Ananya and then she lost consciousness.

"How'd we come here?" She asked and Andrew replied as he entered the room. "I carried both of you here. Man, it was so tough to keep your wounds out of water and not drown. I had to hijack a Chinese lifeboat for that. Anyways doc, how're they?"

"Captain seems all right and would be discharged as soon as her blood transfusion is complete. About our weapons officer..." The trio looked towards the unconscious Ananya as Dr. Ram continued, "I think she should rest. She had taken a lot of beating, and..."

Amaira nodded, "I agree." Dr. Ram and Andrew were surprised on her statement. "Wasn't she the only one who could man the weapons station?" Andrew asked and she replied, "It's true. But after going out there on an infiltrator mission, I realized that how much taxing they are. For a teen they must be beyond breaking."

The trio looked towards her, mesmerized by the innocent looking face. "Can't believe she is the same fierce fighter who killed an entire ship." Andrew said and Amaira nodded. "Well, you should not take someone at face value."

Ananya's body moved and she opened her eyes with a jerk and sprang into sitting position breathing heavily. Dr. Ram and Andrew immediately went there, followed by Amaira who took support of the IV pole. "What happened!?" The doctor asked but didn't get any response. She continued to breathe heavily while perspiring heavily.

"Oh no! Her wounds opened up." He exclaimed as he saw blood dripping on the back of her dress. The nurses were called to change her dressings while the trio discussed. "I never saw her in such a panicked state. Do you have any clues?" Andrew asked. Dr. Ram and Amaira both knew the reasons but tried to avoid his question.

Andrew gave a glare as the duo made excuses to avoid the question. "I think it's due to the mission? Is that so?" Amaira sighed and gave a cryptic answer, "Yes, but way before this one." The nurses came back and informed the doctor that the dressings have been changed.

The trio went to Ananya's bed to find her completely normal. "Hey kid, why were you in a shock when you woke up?" Ananya replied, "I had a nightmare." There was no change in her expression. He continued, "What was it? Regarding the mission you had."

This time Ananya showed some passive reaction, she was clearly uncomfortable with that. Andrew received tons of glares in the meantime causing him to apologize, "Sorry if you aren't comfortable..." His apology was cut short by Ananya who said, "I was reliving my parents' death. It happens every time, whenever I sleep. And it's one of the reasons I always sleep in odd hours on the deck."

"What do you mean?" Amaira asked and she replied, "Captain, remember my interrogation about the spy. After that, I first slept in my bunk. Divya was the one who woke me up and I attacked her." This was probably the first time she shared all that and her eyes were half filled with tears.

Andrew understood the meaning of all events that happened on that day. It was all a facade to hide her inner weakness. "I understand how you feel. I know how my daughter would feel if she went through all this." Andrew stated.

"I wanted to apologize for getting captured. If I hadn't forgotten the gun, you wouldn't have been shot in the heart. Even if you had that metal plate to protect you, I still owe you an apology." Amaira said, her eyes too had tears. But Ananya smiled, "Captain, you should not be sorry for anything. It's all right. I remember in my first mission with my parents, I had them almost killed thrice. You only did that once and I must admit, you knew what to do at the right moment."

"What did you do to kill all the crewmembers instantly?" Amaira asked and she answered, "I rigged our currency notes. The trigger made the notes send a jolt of current through their bodies and then the paper peeled off, poisoning them." Andrew asked, "What was the first wave of explosions? When did you fit the explosives?"

"When you two were enjoying the tour." Ananya replied. Andrew asked, "So, everything went according to your plan?" Ananya smiled and replied, "My plan ended the moment we stepped on the ship." "What?" The trio shrieked. "Yes, after that it was just reaction to consequences. I just let the events unfold as they should and reacted accordingly. That's how infiltrators work."

Everyone was dumb-struck as she continued, "That's the reason why we're so much versatile. Nothing goes out of order ever." She smiled and everyone burst into a short laughter. "Why did you let those two live?" Andrew asked and Ananya's expression changed to serious. "I didn't think it was wrong of mine to do that."

Amaira understood her dilemma and supported her, "It's okay for you to do that." "But the spies I've met always say that they don't leave behind any proof of their existence behind." Amaira again said, "She's not a spy. Those two will leave behind the legacy that how three individuals destroyed their entire blockade."

Ananya's face lit with surprise as she whispered in Amaira's ear, "How'd you know that?" Amaira replied with a smile, "I thought you did that so that the boy didn't grow up like you. Someone told me that she masters in propaganda. What better way than two sailors from the ship telling the same tale? Morale..." Ananya smirked, "You know you could be a better infiltrator."

Amaira and Ananya were allowed to rest. Amaira's blood transfusion was completed in a few hours and she was discharged. Ananya too wanted an early discharge but Dr. Ram and Amaira stopped her. "We're not in any battle, you can come to the bridge during Battlestation call. Now focus on healing."

"Captain, you remember I said that it's important to know your enemy through culture and language." Ananya asked as Amaira was about to leave. "Yes, I do." She replied before turning around to face her. "It wasn't a bluff. And it's possible that the next engagement could be our final one." She said bowing down her head. Amaira nodded and left the room.

After her blood transfusion was completed, it was dialyzed to purge out the remaining toxin from it. The four naval officers kept visiting her regularly. In a strategic meeting held in the infirmary, Naina asked "You told captain that you think our next engagement could be the last?"

Ananya nodded in agreement as she continued, "Why do you think so?" "Think of it commander, put yourself in the enemy's top brass' shoes. What would you've done if you knew that there's a rogue ship? Send an interception party?" Naina nodded.

"Send stalkers." Naina again nodded in agreement. "Try to fork them off?" She again agreed. "Blockade and cordon them off?" A nod. "What will you do if everything fails?" Naina thought for a while and replied in a grim tone, "Send a carrier strike group. That's the only option left."

Amaira was baffled by the suggestion, "You can't be serious. Sending an entire carrier strike group for a single ship. It's outrageous, no one sane enough will do that." Andrew added, "But captain, no one sane enough would believe that one ship managed to do such things. It's perfectly logical that the next thing we'll face is a carrier strike group."

"But the question remains, how many? I don't think they'll pour all resources in one decisive battle." Arman said and Ananya pondered before answering, "One CSG in the best case scenario." "And worst?" "They have five CSG total and three in the IOR, so..." She didn't complete but everyone got the idea of the worst case scenario.

The doctor arrived a few minutes later and said, "Sorry to disturb you, but we'll have to put her on dialysis." "Not again!" Ananya complained. "What, are you afraid of needles?" Andrew joked and she puffed, "Why shouldn't I be? Moreover the process is heck a lot painful." Dr. Ram sighed, "There's no use of complaining, it's the fastest way to getting the poison out of your blood. See in just three sessions, it went down from 4 mg/L to 7 nano gm/L. This one would surely bring down the poison level to zero."

The five of them left the room as Ananya struggled against the doctor and the nurses. Andrew giggled, "So she is a child after all."

Naina added, "But she's brave enough to go through dialysis thrice in two days. It is said to be a very painful and moreover Dr. Ram said that he cannot do this procedure under anesthesia."

Vivaan turned around to see the nurses restrain Ananya while the doctor inserted the special catherer. "I do think he should do that under anesthesia. It'll save a lot of effort." "No, dialysis for poison requires live feedback in order to change the machine settings if required. After all it's like draining out every single drop of oxygenated blood out of her body, filtering it and sending it back. The catherers for portable dialysis machines are one time use, so Ananya has to go through this pain every time dialysis is required." Naina explained. Amaira sighed unable to believe the amount of pain the little teen has to go through.

13

January 26, 2040: It was India's 90th Republic Day and aboard the Chanakya, Amaira hoisted the flag followed by the entire crew singing the national anthem. The ship was sailing parallel to the Indian Coastline, just outside the Indian waters so as to limit combat in the international waters.

Since their escape from Maldives on January 24th's evening, the ship's maximum cruising speed decreased from 50 knots to 42 knots due to increase in weight as they overloaded the armories with main battery shells and other armaments.

The way was also obstructed by multiple pirate attacks though secondary armaments under AI control were more than enough to turn the paper thin ships into floating wrecks before they could even get close. But still, Amaira decided to limit their speed to 35 knots and keep scanning for any enemy ships.

About 2 in the morning, the crew spotted a sunken ship and upon closer inspection; the deck crew informed the captain that they could see a relatively undamaged reconnaissance helicopter on the ship. A raid team consisting of Andrew and two of his men along with Armory master and Naina, went to scavenge any useful resources and came back with the helicopter and few barrels of fuel.

• • • •

AMAIRA WAS IN HER CABIN while the ship was sailing on shift duties. After the ceremony was concluded at 7 in the morning, she had the crew at high alert. Ananya and Naina's warning about a possible carrier threat was worrying her. She went to the internal comm. and asked Naina for a report on the attempts to contact Porbandar.

"No, we aren't able to contact them. Satellite reception is still not here." Naina's response came. "What despite being so close to the mainland, we are unable to connect to satellite?" Amaira shrieked and wondered, 'Did they pull out our satellites?' "Try Line of Sight communication as soon as we get in range."

Amaira looked at the GPS map of the area and sighed, "We're barely able to use US' GPS, thanks to Lt. Andrew's credentials. But..." She switched off the GPS tab after confirming the route and went to the infirmary. She had her wound dressings changed.

"Hmm...your wounds are getting better but the arm..." Dr. Ram said as he examined her wounds. The waist had healed to full while her knee showed some kind of recovery. "After you get back on land, I suggest bed rest for at least a month for you to get walking around. For the arm, it's better to have a plate inserted. The latest bullet went by your bone."

Amaira however, already knew that as she now suffered immense pain in just moving the arm. As he finished, Amaira asked "How is she?" Dr. Ram scratched his head as he took her to Ananya, who seemed to be asleep. "We managed to purge out the entire poison, but frequent dialysis took its toll on her."

"What do you mean?" Amaira asked. Dr. Ram sat on the visitors chair next to Amaira and explained, "Her blood pressure, for instance has fallen to dangerous level. Right now as you can see, her blood pressure is at 80/65. Her nutrition levels have been falling continuously. Her blood glucose level is at 46."

"Isn't that too low?" "Yes, it is. Dialysis removes all of the blood sugar from body and reduces the flow of blood, resulting in reduction in their levels. And because we had to do four dialyses in only two days, the negative effects added up as well." He sighed as the two of them watched Ananya sleep.

Amaira wanted to talk to her but refrained, "I think it's better if I come later. Let's hope we don't need to disturb her recovery." She stood up for a while and left. "Is she all right?" A voice asked and Amaira turned around in surprise to find Andrew standing there.

"Yeah, she's recovering." Amaira replied and moved away. "Someone's getting close to a crew member. You visit her every day, it could be a weakness." Andrew commented and Amaira turned around, "Why'd you care? You also meet her regularly."

Andrew looked surprisingly at Amaira who answered his doubt, "I am the ship's captain. There's nothing on this ship that goes under my nose." He smiled as he went towards the infirmary, "You're right. But my reasons are a lot more personal."

Andrew went in and had talks with the doctor about Ananya. Half an hour later, he emerged out of the infirmary and stood by the wall near it. 'I feel so bad for her. But should I do that...' He thought looking towards the floor before he began walking to the deck.

* * * *

ABOUT 10 IN THE MORNING, an alarm rang across the ship. Amaira rushed to the bridge and asked immediately upon arrival, "Status report." Arman said, "We have spotted ships on radars. Twelve ships in total at 120 nautical miles." "That close!!!" Amaira gulped and quickly regained control, "What are their types?"

Arman said, "We'll have to wait for a while. As soon as we get in 100 nautical mile range, we can identify them." Amaira nodded and took her position, "All right, slow down to maximum battle speed. All hands to Level one battlestations. Put the weaponry at AI." Naina asked, "Isn't Weapon Officer coming?" "She is not in a state to man her station." Amaira replied as ship began to slow down to 33 knots.

At 10:45, as the mutual distance between he two closed down to 97 nautical miles, Arman said "Captain, we have identifications. Chinese Type 004 Aircraft carrier, two cruisers – Chinese Type 019 and Type 126, three destroyers – two Chinese Type 817 and a Type 420 and four Chinese Type 089C Frigates. Apart from that there seems to be two civilian ships – perhaps logistics and supply."

"A Carrier Strike Group!?" Naina gasped as their worst fear has come true. Before Amaira could say anything Arman added, "Oh crap! Captain, we got launches for three fighter squadrons from the carrier." "They've spotted us!!! Prepare for Anti-Aircraft combat. Defense officer, prepare EMP burst. All deck based CIWS are to be kept ready, shoot down all planes. Use our secondary armaments as well."

Chanakya's all secondary armament turrets changed to AA mode. Divya had the EMP powered up and ready. The three squadrons, each having 14 aircrafts and each aircraft equipped with loads of anti-ship weaponry came closer and closer when they entered firing range within minutes of detection.

All defensive weapons began to fire automatically as the EMPs began to blast out in short bursts each lasting eight seconds before the next wave is fired. The airplanes attack with anti-ship missiles and torpedoes which were effectively neutralized by the EMP before the CIWS destroyed them.

The first wave retreated after exhausting all their weapons and still being able to scratch the deck and add scrap on it. By the time they exited the ships' firing range, six fighters were shot down. The second wave from the carrier was immediately launched as the first wave reached half way.

Amaira immediately ordered, "Damage reports." "We have some minor injury reports from the deck crew due to falling debris, other than that nothing." Divyanshu, the internal communication officer said. "Good, reprogram feeder to all secondary guns. Use HE shells with proximity fuses. Nuclear generators to full power. Go full speed ahead."

Chanakya's speed was increased to 40 knots and went steaming to face the next wave head on. The next wave did the same as well, the fighters came in and launched their missiles which were deactivated by the EMP and killed by AA fire.

· · · ·

ABOARD THE CHINESE carrier, it was informed that the fighter squadrons were unable to cause any damage to the ship by missiles. The captain thought for a while and ordered, "The next squadron will carry unguided rockets and bombs." His subordinates looked at him doubtfully, one of them made courage to ask, "This will risk us against their anti aircraft armaments."

The captain shouted at the officer, "Are you questioning my decision?" The officer stammered, "No...Not at all sir. But we can't risk our best pilots for this." "We can hammer that ship with all our missiles and they won't even scratch it, but if it gets into firing range then we're surely doomed. We'll have to sink it outside its firing range."

As the third wave flew away, the next planes were equipped with heavy contact detonating bombs and unguided rockets. The pilots were explained by the engineers, "These are unguided armaments. Get at least within fifteen nautical miles before releasing them. And try to get some hits on the superstructure."

• • • •

BY THE TIME FOURTH wave launched, the distance between Chanakya and the Chinese ships was only sixty nautical miles. In the bridge of Chanakya, Navya informed "We have submarines on SONAR. Six of them spanning from Blue Sigma 150 to Blue Beta 155." Amaira nodded in agreement and ordered, "Prepare for anti-ship and anti-submarine battle as well. Open fire as soon as we get into range."

The fourth wave came into range and the guns opened fire at the fighters. Though they dodged direct shell hits, many planes were caught in the wall of fire that the proximity fuses on the shells created. As the fighters came nearer and nearer, the firing intensity increased. One of the pilots cursed the captain for the suicide mission. As the distance between the fighter and ship decreased to fifteen nautical miles, he released his payload before the plane was hit by the short range EMP.

"We have incoming bombs and rockets." Divya said. "Didn't the EMP hit them?" Amaira asked and she replied, "No, they seem unguided." "Shoot them down!" "Can't, they're in the blindspot." Amaira sighed and ordered, "Use the magnetic interferers to guide them away." Divya responded in affirmative and powered up the magnetic interferers.

Outside on the deck of the ship, nearly twenty small armored cylinders containing powerful electro-magnets emerged. The entire ship was surrounded by a powerful magnetic field that guided the bombs and rockets away from the ship. The lights of the entire ship began to flicker as the nuclear reactors tried to cope up with the energy requirements of the systems.

Amaira had the interferers shut down immediately as the threat cleared. The guns continued to rain hell on the fighters. As the wave retreated more than twenty planes were shot down. As the wave returned the aircraft carrier began to move westwards, away from its escort ships.

The distance between the ships decreased to thirty nautical miles when Chanakya opened fire with the main guns. "Minefield detected." Navya shouted before multiple explosions rocked the ship. "Damage report." Amaira asked and Divya said, "Minimal damage to armor. Ship integrity at 100%." Divyanshu added, "Many non-combatants are injured. Medical staff is rushing to the injured."

"Repurpose half secondaries for anti ship use. Re-program feeders to AP shells for them." Amaira ordered as the enemy ship moved into the range of secondary guns. The guns fired again but the accuracy was way lower than what Ananya's shooting had. The enemy ships evaded the shells easily but still lost couple of ships.

As the distance decreased to ten nautical miles, both sides shelled each other heavily. The Chanakya absorbed the damaged caused by the small caliber guns of the destroyers and frigates while they evaded the shells using their superior mobility. The missiles launched by the Chinese ships were intercepted by the EMP and Anti-air fire.

"Move through. We'll break through their formation to get towards Porbandar." Amaira ordered when Divya shouted, "Torpedoes to the stern. Nine of them, at Black 4." "What? Evade!!!" Amaira ordered knowing that at that close range even EMP disabled torpedoes will hit.

The ship turned port and but six torpedoes made their marks and hit the ship near the propellers. "Stay on course. Arman any ships or fighter towards the stern." Arman scanned the area repeatedly and finally answered, "No Captain. Negative."

Divyanshu shouted, "Captain, spotters have spotted an ECM airplane flying right above us." Amaira never thought that they'll use an ECM airplane as well. "Switch on the ECCM, shoot down the plane by Iron Dome." Arman switched to ECCM radars and exclaimed, "Can't believe this. We have forty ships on our tail. One aircraft carrier, seven destroyers, six cruisers, twelve frigates, ten corvettes and four supply ships. 30 nautical miles."

The Iron dome missile batteries located near aft turrets sprang into action and launched three interceptor missiles at the Chinese ECM plane turning it into a flying fireball. "Captain, we're unable to get the ship back on course, the rudder's not responding." Vivek the propulsion officer said getting a surprised look.

Divya immediately scanned the ship for damage reports and said, "Captain, the rudder hydraulics have been destroyed. The rudder is stuck Port 30." "Stop the ship." Amaira ordered but by the time it stopped, the ship had turned a full 85 degrees towards the port.

• • • •

ABOARD THE CHINESE Type 006 carrier, Admiral Wang celebrated as the Indian ship finally came to a rest. The ECM airplane hid their movements by blocking their radar towards the stern. "Our friends in the media are also ready. Let's see how it goes on."

• • • •

AMAIRA HAD ORDERED the weapons to stop firing and discussed with the bridge on their next course of action. "Can't we purge the rudder completely and move towards the base?" Amaira asked. Divya responded by looking into Ananya's manual that she gave her before her detention, "We can purge the rudder but that'll mean to purge the entire primary armor."

"Ayush try to contact the Porbandar base again." Naina ordered and Ayush, the external communication officer nodded before returning to his station and trying out every single way of communicating. They were barely 50 nautical miles away from the coast of Porbandar but most long-range or LOS means of communication failed.

"Captain should I try using radio as well." He asked. Naina dismissed the idea, "Don't be a fool. If we use radio, they can easily tap our communications." Amaira interrupted irritated, "Just do it. I am pretty sure they know what we'll be doing." After about two minutes, contact was established.

Porbandar Control Station

The radio operator adjusted frequencies to check for any information by the high command. Suddenly a strange noise attracted his attention; he fine-tuned the radio to catch the signal on a random frequency. As the voice cleared out, he jumped out of his chair in surprise. "This is EXS 105, INS Chanakya. Porbandar Control, do you copy?" The voice said in loop.

He immediately responded in the same frequency. "EXS 105 INS Chanakya, this is Porbandar Control..." Before he could continued, the voice said, "We're stuck in the middle of combat about fifty nautical miles from the coast. Our rudder has been damaged, please send backup." "What...Uh...Um...What's the enemy status?"

"Fifty ships, including two CSGs. Please hurry..." The voice broke, the operator tried to re-contact the ship but failed. He immediately took a copy of the recording and rushed to the Commanding officer of the base. "They made it here?" The CO asked in surprise. "Yes sir, but right now they're being surrounded by two CSGs. We should immediately send them backup."

The CO asked the radio operator to contact them again if possible while he made an announcement, "One of our ships from the Eastern Fleet is stuck fifty nautical miles from here. Every available ship on this port is to be immediately refitted and resupplied. Within one hour, they'll move out to assist the ship."

· · · ·

AMAIRA SIGHED AS THE radio operated notified them of the rescue mission. "We'll have to hold on for one hour on our own." Naina added, "At this rate we'll sink before they arrive." The Chanakya was being rained by double vigor while its armaments fired defensively. The armor began to lose some plates as the incoming ships fired torpedoes on the broadside.

Suddenly, they received a message on an open naval channel. "This is Admiral Wang of the fifth Carrier Strike Group. You're surrounded completely, consider this a last warning. All crew members are to line up on the deck without arms for surrender. Rest assured, you'll be treated as Prisoners-of-war and will be released immediately after hostilities cease. Your safety is my assurance. Indian captain, we shall wait for fifteen minutes after that your ship will be sunk."

The message played in loops and Amaira immediately turned the audio off, "It's the International SOS Channel. They used that to fuel up their propaganda. Damn..." "Captain, what'll we do?" Arman asked.

Sonar scan revealed additional eighteen submarines to the surface ships that remained forty six.

"One against sixty four. An impossible odd." Naina said and Amaira nodded in agreement. "So are you going to surrender, captain?" A voice came from the door of the bridge and Amaira turned to find Ananya coming in with Andrew supporting her in the weakened condition. "You didn't answer me Captain!!! Are you going to surrender?"

14

January 26, 2040: It was 12:30 and five minutes have passed since Admiral Wang's warning and in the bridge of Chanakya, a heated debate had started between Amaira and Andrew. Unbeknownst to them, seven media choppers were reporting the battle, LIVE on TV and Internet.

"So what you're saying is that we surrender. We're barely fifty nautical miles away from port. It'll barely take an hour on your speedy ship." Andrew said, drawing a sharp reaction from Amaira, "You shouldn't even say anything Lieutenant. One against sixty four, that's an impossible odd even with this tech."

Ananya who sat on her station and listened to the cat and mouse fight between the two and sighed, "Can you two really behave like adults?" The two stopped and looked at the little girl. "What do you mean?" "I mean stop fighting and try to think a way out of here. Okay, let's start by accounting for all possible actions."

The duo calmed down and nodded, "First way, we surrender. We'll be held as POWs and would be released as soon as the war ends. But they'll capture our ship and try to use it against us." Amaira said and saw Ananya who jotted down the points.

Andrew said next, "Second way, we fight till the last breath. Your reinforcements will leave about fifty minutes later, there's no way that we can hold on a fight at this intensity for so long. The ship will be set to self destruct as soon as it sinks. It's powered by a nuclear reactor if I am correct so that explosion would take out rest of the Chinese fleet."

Naina came up with the next idea, "We'll try to negotiate our surrender and delay it till reinforcements arrive." Vivaan came next, "We can surrender but set the reactors at super-critical before doing so." Arman came up with the final idea, "We can fight defensively until reinforcements come. We can hold on for that long, I am confident about that."

Andrew asked, "Lieutenant Vivaan, you said reactors how many do you mean?" Vivaan stammered but upon getting a nod from Amaira he said, "This ship has four Vikram class Nuclear Reactors, each rated 400MW." "You gotta be kidding me." Andrew's face flushed with surprise. The Chanakya had a power reactor of 1.6GW more than thrice of USA's largest warship.

Ananya who noted all their points, read them and said, "Now this is what I say..." She explained her plan to the naval officers. The entire bridge was surprised at the dangerously effective plan but since it was better than any of the senior's plan, it was agreed.

• • • •

IT WAS ALMOST 12:40 and Admiral Wang waited at the bridge for any response from the Indian Captain. "Looks like they won't surrender sir?" A junior officer said and Wang looked at the Chanakya with his binoculars, "Maybe? Maybe they're busy in making a collective opinion. Individual surrenders are easy but surrendering a ship is a completely different task."

As the clock ticked past 12:40, he picked the mike to announce resumption of attack when another officer said, "Sir there's activity on the ship's deck." Wang again looked at the ship, noting how well the weapons were hidden though he could see the Iron Dome missile batteries and missile launchers. Near the superstructure, people began to come out slowly one by one.

"So they've surrendered. Good!" Wang smiled to himself and ordered all ships to immediately ceasefire and orders unarmed squadrons to check the ship for any suspicious activity. He looks again through the binoculars when suddenly something shocks him, "You got to be kidding me."

"What happened sir?" The junior officer asks, Wang gave him the binoculars to look. The officer too was left surprised as they see children, teenagers and women with babies lining up among the ship's crew. "So they're using civilians as shields." Suddenly another officer came running and said, "Sir we lost contact with all the submarines."

"What?" He looked again in the binoculars to find nearly twenty men wearing naval uniforms on the deck while people in civilian dresses keep coming out of the door. "They're in the process of surrendering. Naval officers are standing on the deck. Scan the area." The officer with radar scans it to notify only the enemy ship and a faint SONAR signal.

· · · ·

AS SOON AS IT WAS 12:40, Ananya's plan was executed. Non combat staff was told to go on the deck slowly with men wearing naval uniforms. Ananya would use the distraction to snipe off the enemy submarines first by using stealth torpedoes. She also fired a slow dummy torpedo that would only move around periphery of the combat area as long as the propeller lasts.

As soon as the CIC informed that the Chinese destroyers have scrambled to destroy their dummy submarine, Ananya quickly trained all the ship's guns to the starboard. The targeting system locked all the remaining six ships and she fired a full anti-ship broadside on them.

"Hurry up everyone, quickly now go to the life boats. Drop them on the starboard side." Divyanshu made the announcement and the people quickly ran to the life boats. All Chinese ships there sank leaving only the forty portside ships.

"How predictable." Ananya sighed as she held her head by her hand. "We'll commence cover fire." Amaira ordered and everyone nodded. The Chinese ships on the other side began to fire as well. The gunfire overwhelmed the defenses and within ten minutes Divya complaint, "I am not getting enough power to run all the defensive systems at full power."

Amaira ordered, "Redirect power from useless compartments to defensive units. Hurry up with the evacuations." Ananya fired the weapons in suppressive fire mode for anti-aircraft. Suddenly an aircraft plunged on top of the ship's superstructure. "EMP failing. An aircraft crashed into the EMP device." Divya informed.

"Divert EMP's power to rest of the armaments. Ananya fire on the enemy ships." Amaira ordered and Ananya began to fire on the enemy ships. "Torpedoes on the broadside." Divya shouted but with EMP gone, their torpedo protection was almost nil. "Identify the armor plates to be hit. And purge them immediately after hits." Amaira ordered. 'We've to compromise our armor for protection.'

• • • •

ON THE CHINESE CARRIER, Wang was left baffled by the tactic the Indian ship took. "What's taking you so long to disable the ship?" "Sir, it looks like we've disabled the thing that was shutting our missiles down." An officer replied. "Fire at the main guns."

All the Chinese ships began to dodge the accurate multi-vector fire while focusing their fire on the main guns. The HE shells exploded on impact but unable to cause any damage or start fire. The officer reported back to Wang, "Sir HE shells are unable to cause any damage. The turrets are heavily armored." Wang ordered, "Switch to AP shells and continue the missile and torpedo barrage."

The ships now numbering thirty five, focused their Armor Piercing salvos on the armored turrets. But the shells bounced off the turrets harmlessly. "This is crazy." Wang cursed as he saw the shells bounce off the turrets instead of destroying it.

• • • •

"IT'S JUST LIKE WE PLANNED. They're targeting the magnetically armored turrets, giving us a clear path for damage control." Amaira said and asked Divyanshu, "What about our repair work?" He replied, "The maintenance team has transplanted all starboard armor plates on port side. Our port side has double reactive armor strength."

Suddenly the ship began to tilt starboard, "Captain, we're listing starboard." Naina exclaimed and Amaira ordered, "Flood all port ballast tanks." All port ballast tanks were filled with water and the ship's tilting slowed before stopping and going back straight. "Now we can hold a little longer."

Ananya asked the armory personnel about ammunition status. "We still have ammunition for two hours of intense firing." Ananya pulled back slowly and said, "We're good to go." Volleys of missiles came in, but the magnetic interferers slowed them down long enough for the CIWS and other guns to shoot them down.

"Captain, I am firing concussion missile at the bow aircraft carrier." Ananya said and Amaira nodded, "Permission granted." Three concussion missiles were fired at the Type 004 carrier. The fighters and the CIWS aboard the carrier shot down the missiles but the micro missiles embedded in them hit the surface destroying all other planes and the runway as well.

The battle continued for more than an hour with the Chinese forces now reduced to seventeen while the Chanakya only had a single layer of its special reactive armor that helped it endure such a punishment for so long. Divya gave Amaira the next damage report, "We only have sixty armor plates left. Hull integrity is at 10%, we're listing port at 12 degrees."

Arman shouted, "Captain, reinforcements are here. Twenty nautical miles starboard." Ayush connected the comm. link to the reinforcements' flagship, INS Himgiri. "INS Chanakya, please respond." Amaira began the conversation on an encrypted line, "This is the captain of INS Chanakya." "Please hold in there, we're trying to reach you as soon as possible."

Amaira stopped them, "No, please conduct a rescue mission over there. Our life boats carrying civilians from Camorta have been released over an hour ago, they'll be there by now." "What about you?" "We'll hold the line as long as we can, our rudder's damaged so we're just a sitting duck."

"Don't push your luck; we'll be there as soon as we're done here." The captain of INS Himgiri said before the communication line snapped. Amaira thought for a while and said as the ship was being battered by the missiles, bombs, rockets and missiles, "This might be my final order as the Captain." She took the internal communication mike and order, "ALL HANDS, ABANDON SHIP!!!"

The crew members protested against the order. But Amaira stayed adamant on the order and said, "You all leave, I'll provide the cover fire." Naina protested, "Captain this is absurd. We aren't leaving this ship." "Please don't burden me anymore. I know these nine days have been extremely daunting but please this is my last order as the Captain."

Naina, Arman and Vivaan tried their best to persuade her otherwise but failed. In the meanwhile, they had the drafted crew members evacuate. When Andrew and the Americans came in the bridge, the four of them were still arguing while Ananya managed the guns. "Captain Amaira, would you mind telling why you ordered abandonment of ship now?"

Amaira answered to Andrew, "Our reinforcements have arrived and our reactive armor's all but gone. A single torpedo can now effectively sink us. I cannot risk my crew members for this. What are you doing here? That order is equally applicable to you guys as well."

"You might have the seniority but we're not in the Indian Navy. We can man this ship through the final phase, after all our ship was sunk days prior by a missile." Andrew replied getting a mad reaction from Amaira. The argument over the abandonment order escalated when they noticed that Ananya kept the guns firing in order to keep the Chinese at bay.

"Huh...geez. The barrels have overheated. Looks like we need to take a break or else they're going to pop out. Are you guys finished?"

Ananya sighed. Amaira giggled and immediately changed expression to serious before asking "Why didn't you evacuate?" "You guys were busy fighting among each other, so I used the time to keep the enemy at bay so that they don't sink this ship while you're having this discussion." Ananya said as she slowly got up.

As Ananya began to move towards the door, Amaira explains to others "Don't worry, it'll take only upto twenty minutes before the reinforcements complete their rescue mission. So..." She couldn't complete as Ananya hit her in the back with all her strength shrieking, "Ouch..." Amaira fell forward unconscious and was held by Ananya who painfully asked, "Can someone grab her fast?"

Naina, Arman and Vivaan caught her, relieving Ananya of the weight. "Why'd you do that?" Ananya answered to the bewildered officers, "You should hurry up and get to the life rafts. They aren't firing on us right now." Vivaan asked, "What about you?" "In this condition, I'll be more of a liability if I go out. It'll be better if I stay here and be of some use." She said as she took support of the nearby wall breathing heavily.

"Go before they damage any of the remaining lifeboats." The officers nodded and quickly moved out leaving her alone on the bridge. Vivaan stayed behind and asked, "Why don't you go? We can put the weaponry on AI for cover fire." Ananya smiled as she crawled to her station. "We don't have much ammunition left. It's important now to fire the weapons manually."

"Then save yourself, let any one of us be the last one." He protested as Ananya charged the weapon capacitors to enable ultra-long range mode. "It would be a waste if any of you dies for such a reason." "Huh...What do you mean?" He asked as she continued, "You are far more valuable to the nation than someone like me. Now go..."

She pushed Vivaan out of the bridge and locked the bridge. "Take my belongings as well, tell captain that it's a gift from me." She said and added in a low tone, "Just like mom gifted them to me."

Vivaan was the last one to board the life raft amidst the heavy shelling. The armored deck was now a mess full of holes and shrapnel pieces. He looked at the main turrets that fired 16 inch shells turning red hot due to the explosions. "Hurry up Lieutenant." Naina shouted as they lowered the raft into the ocean leaving one for Ananya.

"Hey, look up there." An American soldier pointed up in the sky. Six to Seven media helicopters were flying over them. "So everything was propaganda." Andrew said, gritting his teeth as they distanced from the Chanakya. He remembered how the ship looked when it came to rescue them and now it was still there fighting off the enemies till its last breath.

The Indian reinforcements arrived from the opposite side and rescued them. Amaira was immediately sent to the infirmary while rest of them were given blankets and water. "Who's the in-charge?" A high ranking officer asked. Naina replied, "Captain Amaira had been taken to the infirmary."

"Oh, what happened?" Naina looked here and there on the question, "She was knocked unconscious due to an explosion near her while evacuating." The officer said, "I am Rear Admiral Neeraj Gautam. It's a pleasure to meet you. We almost gave up hopes of any ship surviving the three pronged attack on Camorta. And who're they?" He pointed towards Andrew and his group.

Andrew moved forward offering a hand-shake "I am Andrew Gibbs, Lieutenant Commander of USS Philadelphia of the Third Reconnaissance Fleet. And we are what remain of the fleet." Naina looked around to see many injured people on board with many dead bodies. "What happened to them?"

Rear Admiral Neeraj responded, "When they were in the life rafts, the Chinese soldiers opened fire on them from their rafts. They returned fire and then Chinese planes snooped in with their auto-cannons. We got two rafts with no survivors and three with major injuries to the people." They gritted their teeth as they turned to see that the Chanakya almost killed off the enemy fleet but it was listing at 15 degrees.

"Is someone on the ship?" He asked and Vivaan replied, "Yes, a crew member volunteered to stay back when Captain was injured. She was supposed to come out in the last life raft as soon as the ship's ammunition was over." He completed the statement to see the last life raft coming through.

The people on board reveal themselves to be the armory personnel. Arman asked the armory master, "Where's the weapon control officer?" The armory master nodded in negative when a portion of Chanakya's bridge collapsed and the ship began to move. "Form patrol parties, chase down the ship and capture it. Looks like the enemy got it, keep a safe distance."

15

Volgograd, Russia

A G-7 meeting was being held in Volgograd on January 26, 2040. It was mutually agreed for the Russian Federation to be the host. Along with the top leaders of the G-7 nations, leaders of The Republic of India and People's Republic of China were also there. The agenda of the meeting was a ceasefire agreement between the two warring countries.

At 11:30 am local time, the Chinese President Rin Cha-Tea began as the break ended "This is the final proposal from the People's Republic of China for a ceasefire. Both countries' armies will hold their positions and a de-facto border will be created. After that all third party countries will be set free. That includes Nepal, Bhutan, Myanmar and Sri Lanka from our side and Pakistan and Maldives from your side."

Indian Prime Minister Ayushya Verma immediately rejected the idea, "No. The proposal from our side is that both countries' armies will return to their pre 1949 positions." Rin immediately countered, "Given your pathetic situation, you are not in any state to bargain. Quietly accept whatever we offer."

"Mind your language, Chinese President Rin." He responded drawing a sharp reaction from Russian President Ivan Dmitri, "Can't you two go on without fighting? This is an informal meeting with no media coverage but it's too much. We're sick of your fighting, decide how you're going to cease hostilities or else we'll be forced to go to UN for this."

Rin stood up and said, "Indian forces are losing at all sides and we hold complete supremacy in all aspects. Still you capitalist nations refuse to see the inferiority of your systems. India should surrender." Italian Prime Minister Ginevra Giorgia supported the Chinese President, "Coming to think of it Prime Minister Verma, the deal is not bad. They're giving up claims on three countries while you're doing it on two."

US President John West added, "I think both of you should accept the status quo. Keep the annexed countries as well." China however immediately rejected the offer. The political impasse continued for fifteen minutes when Chinese Ambassador came in and whispered something to President Rin.

"I am proposing an unconditional Indian surrender to China. We'll sieze all of India's nuclear weaponry and..." Rin was interrupted by PM Verma who asked, "Who gave you the authority to decide that?" Rin smiled and said, "After seeing this, these friends of yours will also say this."

She turned on the LED screen mounted on the wall and switched to a Chinese news channel. "Look at this." The news anchor said something in Chinese and switched to footage, it showed a ship with big naval guns surrounded by multiple other small ships. The surrounded ship had an Indian flag hoisted on the mast while the surrounding ones had Chinese flags.

"I don't believe this crap, this is some of your pesky propaganda." PM Verma said and Rin smirked, "Then how about some of your friends' channel." She changed the channel to CNN, BBC, CNBC and Al Jazeera – all showing the same news footage. US president John West asked to stay on CNN or BBC. The BBC presenter said:

· · · ·

"WE HAVE THIS LIVE FOOTAGE courtesy our international team. This naval battle is being fought about fifty nautical miles off the coast of Gujarat where Indian Navy has the largest stronghold. According to the sources, this ship was part of a fleet but when they were attacked by the Chinese ships the smaller fast ships managed to get away while the big guy got caught.

The Indians were outnumbered one to five and it is reported that the captain of this ship stayed behind to provide cover-fire. Now it is outnumbered one to forty six. The fleet admiral just has given a universally translated message through the International SOS channel to the captain of Indian ship. Let's hear that."

"This is Admiral Wang of the fifth Carrier Strike Group. You're surrounded completely, consider this a last warning. All crew members are to line up on the deck without arms for surrender. Rest assured, you'll be treated as Prisoners-of-war and will be released immediately after hostilities cease. Your safety is my assurance. Indian captain, we shall wait for fifteen minutes after that your ship will be sunk."

"So let's head over to our analyst, Mr. Von Braun. Mr. Braun! Would you like tell us about the situation the Indian captain would be now facing." The camera turned to another man sitting in the same studio with the anchor. "It is one of the situations that no one would like to fall in. The ship is heavily out-numbered and in this situation, surrendering looks like a lucrative offer. But practically speaking, it is a very difficult decision and I am pretty sure that the Captain would instead go for an all out battle."

"Thanks Mr. Von Braun. We must now wait for fifteen minutes before knowing what the Indian Captain does. We can now proceed to our reporter Millie Milder, who's reporting live from the battlefield. Millie, can you tell us what the situation on ground is?"

The camera shifted to another woman who seemed to be standing near the edge of a helicopter "Thanks Sarah, I must tell our viewers that right now we're at a height of 500 feet from combat surface and it is very dangerous here. Chinese fighters from the carriers are speeding by us at supersonic speeds."

The camera focused on the outside to show multiple fighters going around the place. "As you can see, we're getting a good look at the Indian big guy and you gotta admit, it is a perfect war-machine." The anchor who now had half of the screen said, "Please update us with any ground development."

About ten minutes later, the reporter said "Sarah, the deadline is arrived and we've almost no action from the Indian side. Looks like getting full ship surrender is a very tedious task. No, wait I can see something on the deck. I am requesting the cameraman to please focus on the deck near the ship's superstructure."

The camera zoomed in to show people coming out of the ship one-by-one. "Looks like the captain has decided to go for surrender. Sarah look...zoom in...zoom in..." The camera further zoomed and the helicopter lowered to show people and children in civilian dresses coming out as well. "Looks like the ship was ferrying civilians as well and..."

The Chinese destroyers began to move on both sides of the Indian ship. "Sarah, looks like the Chinese side has accepted the surrender and is going to board the ship. No..." Her voice was muffled by the loud explosive sound of the twelve guns firing at once on the six ships that were clubbed together.

"Whoa, Sarah I don't think you'll believe what I saw. There were six ships standing over there..." The reporter said as the camera moved towards the six ships that exploded live. The anchor replied, "Yeah, we are seeing that." The camera came back to the ship as the people gathered on the deck ran to the life rafts.

The life rafts landed on the opposite side while the guns quickly traversed on the Chinese side and opened fire. "This is crazy, what is the captain thinking?" The guns fired continuously in fifteen second intervals and the Chinese ships scrambled to avoid the fire while returning fire.

The camera shifted back to the studio where the expert analyzed the event. "This is going to be a very controversial decision. The captain utilized the civilians as shields to distract the enemy to catch them off-guard and now the ship is acting as a shield to protect the civilians. He really used some brain and guts."

The anchor asked, "What do you think would be next?" "I think the captain is thinking of supporting the life rafts until either they sink or the reinforcements arrive. As you can see, the ship is listing and correcting that means that flooding has begun. If I were in such a case in a surrounded ship with civilians, as a captain my priority would be to safeguard all the civilians and try to keep them away from combat."

The reporter interrupted as the anchor was about to ask the expert, "We have Indian reinforcement ships at the horizon. They're picking up the life rafts. And look at the barrels of the Indian ship's guns, they're red hot and smoking. Both sides have stopped firing and the Chinese ships are trying to group up. It looks like an endgame. I can only see about fifteen ships on the Chinese side as compared to forty six when the battle started an hour ago."

The expert commented, "Looks like the ship is extremely heavily armed and armored with extensive compartmentalization. Looks like the Indians made this big guy especially for blockade breaking." The anchor asked, "Are you suggesting that this is an anti blockade ship, Mr. Von Braun." "It's a good name but I think a blockade breaker would be a better name. Now for the viewers who may not know this term, a blockade is a tactical arrangement of ships such that they don't let any other ships, small or large to enter."

"Millie, is there any further developments?" The anchor asked the reporter who responded, "It looks like the Indian bug guy ran out of ammunition. And the Chinese side seems to be well aware of that. They are cautiously moving towards the Indian ship and..." The reporter's video paused and resumed after a second's lag.

"Looks like they're abandoning the ship. As you could probably see, many people wearing naval uniforms are rushing towards the remaining life rafts. Wait, if you look closely, don't they seem too young to be naval officers?" The camera zoomed at the rushing people with many looking like teenagers when the secondary guns of the ship opened fire at the aircrafts.

The screen switched back to the expert who commented, "What we're seeing right now could be a blatant violation of all international laws of war from both sides." As the parallel screen showed the Chinese fighters scooping low and shooting the life-rafts with their guns. As the anti-aircraft armaments spewed a wall of fire, fighters began to fall like flies.

The anchor said, "Would you explain how this is a violation of war laws? "The Indian side has children manning their warship while the Chinese side is attacking the defenseless sailors in the sea." The reporter interrupted, "Sorry to disturb but we have an interesting update. The main guns have spilt and we now an even longer armament is formed."

The video showed the main guns of the ship split and two rails coming out extending into air. A loud bang followed by violent shaking of the camera occurred as the reporter spoke, "Whoa...Hey focus over there! Focus over there! I would like to show the audiences the explosions that are occurring on the aircraft carriers due to the warheads hitting it."

"The warhead went through two ships completely before hitting the aircraft carrier. It completely penetrated the ships and they are being abandoned. Look at the wave this round caused." The camera shifted a little lower from the ships to show the massive waves generated by the shock wave of firing.

The naval expert was left in awe by the footage and said, "I wanted to see this epic battle by my two eyes." "Indeed Mr. Braun, but would you mind telling our audiences what happened right now?" "Uh...Um" He cleared his throat as he replied, "Well to let everyone know, naval shells are built so that they arm themselves only after a certain velocity reduction. Say, for example if a shell is made to detonate at a speed let's say 10m/s, so it won't detonate before the velocity of the shell is reduced to that level."

He picked up the glass of water and drank some before continuing, "This mechanism helps them to pierce the strongest of armor. The higher is the velocity, the higher is the penetration. This however has a downside, if the thing it is hitting let's say the enemy ship fails to reduce the velocity to that level then the warhead can simply go through. In the footage we saw, the initial shell velocity was so high that it penetrated two warships and a column of water before the velocity lowered enough to arm the explosive charge."

"Can you please provide us a rough estimate of the initial shell velocity?" The anchor asked. "Hmm...going by the penetration and the

wave formation. It must be at least Mark 8, i.e. eight times the speed of sound." The anchor's face flushed with awe, "It could easily overtake the world's fastest fighter."

"The Chinese ships are being abandoned. There is a massive explosion just below the carrier deck. Looks like it's a complete turn-around. And the final life raft from the Indian ship is lowered. Now we can say that this ship is..." She couldn't continue as the Indian ship began to move forward. "...Not abandoned. Sarah look, the Indian side is forming patrol parties to catch up to the ship."

The screen now showed the helicopter footage as it chased the Indian ship from a safer distance while the Chinese fighters attacked the superstructure with all their might. "There's a lone carrier in front of the ship that was disabled in a missile attack by the Indian ship. Looks like it's going to complete an old business."

The distance between the ships decreased rapidly though the Chinese carrier tried to outmaneuver the pursuer. "As you can see that this Indian big fella is very fast. We're moving at around 85 kmph to keep up with the Indian ship and..." Again her voice was muffled as the front six guns opened fire at Chinese carrier.

"The carrier has stopped moving, looks like the shells hit something important." The reporter said as the anchor asked, "Would tell the approximate distance between the two ships, Millie." As another bang from the guns went through, the reporter said "I can't say for sure but it's nearly thirty kilometers or so, and by the speed difference both ships should meet in fifteen to twenty minutes."

"Thank you Millie, Please update us with any important developments." The anchor said and the screen switched to the anchor and the expert in the studio. "Mr. Von Braun, would like to tell us your new views about the Indian behemoth."

"Well, about what I am seeing now I think it would be better to double check our sources. There's a lot of contradicting material available. A slow ship moves at 85 kmph, a surrounded and almost surrendered vessel takes

out all enemy ships. The Indians who supposedly fled came for rescue." He said surely displaying annoyance.

"Indeed. Let's get to Millie if she can get any further update on the situation." The anchor said and the screen shifted to the reporter's view. "The distance between the ships is closing and now as you can see the Indian ship has begun firing at the Chinese ship. The shots are hitting very accurately and Oh My God!!!" The camera wobbled as she muttered the words.

"What happened Millie? Are you all right?" The anchor shrieked as the camera stabilized as the reporter replied, "An interceptor missile just brushed past us. The pilot performed some evasive maneuvers. I was saying that look at the trajectory of the Indian ship; it's on a collision course. Looks like the captain has decided to ram the Chinese carrier."

The camera showed as the airplanes continued attacking using missiles, the bridge crumbled and collapsed on itself after an explosion right under it. "The bridge of the Indian ship has collapsed. It doesn't looks like someone was there and the ship isn't slowing down nor ceasing the attacks."

A few minutes later, the camera footage showed as the two ships came in close proximity and the Chinese evacuating their carrier. "They are now very close and look, the Chinese are abandoning their carrier. The fire from the Indian ship has left the deck completely disfigured but looks like it couldn't get much deep. And..."

The reporter went silent as the two ships collided at high speed. The Indian ship's front went through the Chinese ship easily like a hot knife through butter. The hull deformed as the ship went through and through the carrier with decreased speed. It stopped halfway and both ships began to capsize.

The anchor looked stunned by what she saw and immediately stood up, clapping. The expert too, followed suit. "This is perhaps the bravest moment I ever saw in my life." The expert, Mr. Von Braun remarked as he wiped a tear from his cheek. Millie the reporter continued, "Sarah, the

Indian patrols have got here finally and the big ships are following them. They are rescuing the Chinese sailors, perhaps to capture them as POWs."

16

Volgograd, Russia

The entire meeting was stunned by the battle. The bravery and insanity of the Indian captain had left them wondering, 'What the hell just happened? Is it even possible?' "Now what?" PM Verma sighed as President Rin rose and said, "So, what did you do? How the hell did you give this botched tape to all the international news agencies?"

PM Verma smiled and said, twisting his chair, "Gentlemen, I think we should end our talks about the ceasefire and instead begin a discussion on an unconditional Chinese surrender." The G-7 leaders discussed the matter for a few minutes. PM Verma had a comfortable smile, first since the meeting convened; on his face.

"We can have a vote on that." UK PM Bill Hastings said. President Rin however protested, "I don't know how you believe that propaganda video perpetrated by India." US President John West immediately pointed out, "One, that video was presented by you not India. Two, that wasn't any propaganda..."

Italian PM Ginevra Giorgia asked, "How're you so sure about that? No inquiry was conducted about that, maybe they have provided this video material to all news agencies." President John responded, "That was live. And everything that the reporter said must've happened in real time. I agree to the voting proposal."

The eight representatives – United States, United Kingdom, France, Germany, Italy, Japan, Canada and Russia; begin an oral vote. The results were in favor of an informal discussion with seven to one majority. Only Italy dissented. Canadian Prime Minister Menander Singh asked, "Prime Minister Ayushya Verma, would you tell what your demands for surrender are?"

PM Verma said, "Both countries would move their armies to pre 1949 positions. China's entire nuclear arsenal will be destroyed in the presence of UN and Indian forces. One China Policy and CPEC will be considered non-existent. The assets of People's Republic of China, including their shares and the shares of companies registered under PRC will be sold off to pay the war remedies to India and other countries involved voluntarily or involuntarily."

President Rin immediately rejected the proposal, "We won't surrender. We're winning the war, you can't force us to surrender based on a botched up video. It's you who should surrender to our superior civilization and military." PM Verma who was already irritated with her interruptions and statements said, "I was trying not to get involved in any more bloodshed. But if you want then the Indian Armed Forces will make you do that."

Before anyone could say anything, he called his Ambassador and asked her to make a call to the CDS. The Ambassador took out a strange looking mobile phone and called the CDS. "Just for the Chinese President's solace, I am putting the conversation on speaker."

"Jai Hind, Prime Minister Sir." The voice from the other side said. "Jai Hind, CDS Subhash Mukherjee. Do you know anything about the ship aforementioned in the international media?" "Sir, it is one of the ships that were stationed in Camorta before the assault. It is listed as one of the major sunken ships. Sir, what are your orders?" The CDS replied to PM Verma.

"The talks regarding ceasefire have failed. All Indian troops will advance into Chinese Territory to annex them, until further orders. We're officially at war." PM Verma ordered and the CDS replied, "Ok sir. Jai Hind!" "Jai Hind!" And he ended the call, handing over the phone to the Ambassador who immediately snapped the phone in two.

Within minutes, one by one Ambassadors of all G-7 nations came in with phone calls from their intelligence chiefs. "Let's meet after an hour." Russian President Ivan Dmitri said and the members left the meeting room.

The meeting resumed at 2:00 pm and President Ivan began, "Our intelligence agencies have confirmed that all BMLs in the Indian subcontinent have been activated." President John displayed the Indian subcontinent's map on the LED screen and said, "CIA has confirmed that hostilities have been renewed all over the combat zone. In the west, Chinese forces are now defending the CPEC – their last bastion and trade route from artillery and air force. And in the east, Indians have broken the Chinese blockade of Vishakhapatnam."

Germany's Chancellor Hillary Mendel asked, "What was that battleship in the footage?" "I too, know only that much what you know. It was one of the ships that were stationed in Camorta, the former HQ of Indian Navy's Eastern Fleet before the Chinese attacked it in midst of a communication blackout."

PM Verma called his Ambassador and asked, "Get us some information about that ship." "Right away sir!" She went to a corner and called someone. Upon completing the conversation, she came back and whispered into PM Verma's ear. "Tell it to all. It's endgame already." She whispered back, "Are you sure sir?"

PM Verma nodded and she replied, "It was one of the prototypes that we were testing before the war. It had been pushed into active duty with the onset of the war. One of the perfected anti-fleet types." "One of the...Do you mean that there are more?" President John asked and she again looked at PM Verma, "Sorry sir, but this is out of my league. I can't reveal that."

PM Verma sighed, "All right. It was supposed to be a mass produced assault ship. If my memory serves correct, we were supposed to induct six of them this year and three in the next year. Tell me if I am wrong." The Ambassador looked at the PM and nodded, "No sir. You're right, but due to the war situation their final sea trials were hastened and I am told that we have seven of them in combat ready situation waiting for orders to launch them. The rest of them will be ready for combat in three to four weeks."

President Ivan smirked, "Seven of these behemoths could even sink the entire People's Liberation Army's Navy. If we go by the performance we saw in the battle, I think even three will do." "He's bluffing. No one would be such a fool to keep these powerhouses hidden when needed the most." The little smile on President Rin's face vanished as PM Verma ordered, "Ambassador Shreya, inform all our Defense Companies involved in the ship's manufacturing. I want all ships to be rolled out within three weeks. Have the CDS assign a small escort fleet to those ships who'll sail to South China sea and engage in demolition of all Chinese ports and Chinese military installations near it."

The ambassador nodded and left. PM Verma sat down and smiled, "You'll see for yourself what kind of bluff it is." The Chinese President visibly went cold but stayed adamant that they have the upper hand not the Indians. About 3:30 pm, the meeting was adjourned for the day and the leaders went out for a press statement.

A reporter asked, "Sir, what are the views of G-7 on the new offensive by the Indian forces?" "We're on a wait and watch strategy. The naval battle in the Arabian Sea had changed the dynamics of the situation completely. And based on the discussion we had, it is decided that Indian actions won't be responded as long as the conflict is localized." US President responded.

Another reporter asked the Chinese President, "We all saw the footage in which a single Indian ship defeat multiple fleets of your Navy. Don't you think it would be better if you agree to a ceasefire?" President Rin tried her best to maintain cool and said, "That was a botched up video by the Indian Propaganda Machine. We're still having advantage in all sectors."

She left the platform in the middle refusing to talk to the media. "This war will be soon over." PM Verma said as he left the platform as well leaving the host Russia and G-7 leaders to deal with the media. The leaders too left the platform after a few minutes of talk.

January 27, 2040

The next day, talks convened at 10:00 am. Russian President Ivan began the talks by giving a showing a satellite report of the ground events. "Yesterday's day was quite hectic for the armed forces. That news clip was verified by independent Russian analysts to be original. Our reconnaissance aircrafts flew over the area to verify the events." He displayed a picture taken by the reconnaissance plane; it showed the half submerged bridge of the Indian ship and parts of the carrier.

"We can also show you detailed satellite images of the area." PM Verma interrupted and showed the satellite images, showing the debris of the Chinese ships sunk by the super-ship as well. President Rin asked, "We destroyed all your military and communication satellites before going for the attack on your naval HQ. How'd you get these satellite images?"

"Courtesy of our Israeli friends. Anyways, as for battle progress..." He switched the images to show the military movements in an animation. "Bangladesh has given access to Indian Armed Forces through their territory. We have managed to recapture Sikkim. Up north, our forces were waiting outside Lhasa and now have captured Tibet's capital."

"Watch your words Prime Minister Verma; you are undermining the 'One China Policy'." Rin shouted but PM Verma ignored her completely and continued, "CPEC and Pakistan have fallen. Nepal will be liberated soon." "Huh...You would never beat us. These are just tactical victories, just like the saying 'Losing a battle to win a war'. Even the Soviet Union had to retreat against Hitler's Nazi Germany only to strike back."

PM Verma gave a sour look, "You only have Nepal because your forces are hiding in Mt. Everest's cover. Let's see if the Himalayas can save you from the wrath of Indian Army." President Ivan Dmitri verified the claims, "The Indians are in quite an advantageous position. However, China still claims majority of its South China Sea based assets."

The US Ambassador rushed in to the President with a phone. "Excuse me." President John said as he got p from the seat and went outside the conference room to take the call. He came back after a few minutes, took his seat and asked calmly, "President Rin Cha Tea of People's Republic of China. I want you to give me a reason why shouldn't I declare war on China."

"What do you mean by that?" She asked. "I just got a call from my military chief. The United States' Third Reconnaissance Fleet was destroyed in a surprise Chinese missile attack in the IOR. Now give me a reason why I shouldn't declare war on China or have you arrested for the massacre of thousands of American sailors." US President John yelled fiercely.

However, Rin sighed completely overlooking the colossal loss. "What the hell was your fleet doing in a battle zone without informing the Chinese Navy? It's almost legitimate that any shore bound missile defense system would pick it up as an enemy ship." "For your information, we were in the international waters far away from your Hambantota port. Some of our sailors were rescued, thanks to our Indian friends and they said that the ship that rescued them detected a missile boat towards your precious port."

Rin stood up enraged, stomping on the ground "You should learn to keep your nose out of others business." President John stood up and shouted, "Are you threatening me? Remember that we can level your entire country just like that ship leveled your carrier and I promise when we do, there won't be any survivors or prisoners."

Rin smirked, "Oh yeah, it'll take you more than a week to get your forces ready since our deal with Taiwan. I'll end this war with a strategic Chinese dominance, today itself..." She called the Chinese Ambassador, who came in with a black briefcase. She immediately opened it and brought out a key from her pocket.

The ambassador combined her key with his own and put it in a keyhole inside the briefcase. Japanese Prime Minister Sugou Kawachi stood up and shouted, "DON'T YOU EVEN DARE TO LAUNCH NUKES. THE FUTURE GENERATIONS WON'T FORGIVE YOU FOR THIS ENDEAVOR." The statement lost every last form of diplomacy or mannerism and could be considered a serious threat.

Rin however howled in pride, "The so-called future generations forgave the US for Hiroshima and Nagasaki. This event will mark the end of this conflict and no one will ever question China's might." PM Sugou immediately called his Ambassador and ordered him, "Prepare all interceptors. Shoot down Chinese missiles as soon as they get into air."

The entire meeting looked towards him with surprise but he stayed defiant, refusing to take back the orders. "Prime Minister Sugou, you do realize that you're escalating the conflict from a regional one to a theatre one." President John said and PM Sugou responded, "I don't care about escalations. I won't let any other country suffer our fate of 1945."

PM Verma immediately stood up and yelled, "I had enough of this. You want to escalate this into a nuclear war, so be it." He called Ambassador Shreya with his own briefcase. "Call the NSA and tell him to have the Kavach interceptors ready to fire." Both leaders pushed the switch almost simultaneously.

President Ivan switched the screen to satellite images as it showed missiles from different BMLs launched. Japanese interceptors helped India and China both to intercept the nuclear missiles. Chinese launchers due to their relative safe location on the East Coast were primary targets for the Japanese interceptors.

But Indian missiles were launched and targeted locations far off from the range of Japanese interceptors. Chinese interceptors scrambled to intercept the Indian missiles, succeeding in taking care of most of the long range ones. The short range missiles mostly aimed at the military bases in Nepal and Qinghai, Gansu and Eastern Tibetan provinces of China got through the defenses before they could be prepared.

For fifteen minutes, a dead silence draped the room. The Chinese president slumped into her chair, unable to believe that she overlooked such a point. Japan had suffered nuclear apocalypse and due to its survivor's trauma, it would do anything in its power to not let any other nation face it.

President John broke the silence and said, "This is enough. This petty war of yours is now over. We're calling an emergency UNSC meeting and a combined Russian – NATO force will be deployed to mediate between the two armies." The member nations stood one-by-one in agreement. President John continued, "So this is our unanimous decision that all conflict would be..."

However, he was unable to finish as his Ambassador came in with latest satellite feed from NASA. The Satellite feed showed the different desperate last stands of the Chinese military in different sectors. Most videos showed as many frontline soldiers held their positions while the military bases were evacuated.

"Our society!" President Rin exclaimed. Many scholars and think tanks around the world have expressed their concerns about the recent uprisings and their brutal suppression in China. As the President, Rin was warned multiple times about the imminent collapse of the Chinese society that could be brought upon by almost any incident.

The Chinese expansionist policies were meant to be a curb and lid on the nation's heated youth. The energy of the youth was channeled into the bloody two year war with India. And now, those Indians; who were ridiculed in China as barbarians and lowly were bringing that society to a collapse.

For years, it was the brought up Chinese mentality that anytime the two countries will go on a conflict, history (1962) will repeat itself. But the enlightenment to harsh reality was anything but acceptable, not only did the supposed inferior nation held its own against China who used all available resources but now was pushing into Chinese territory with remarkable speed.

The Japanese Ambassador rushed in and whispered something in PM Sugou's ear. The two had a brief talk, following which the Japanese PM announced, "Our intelligence agents have confirmed that Hong Kong has fallen to the combined Indo-Taiwanese forces. The Indian forces are squeezing the Chinese military from all sides."

"What?" President Rin shouted, her expression showing that the final fuse has blown up. "This can't be!!!" She murmured as she confirmed the news from her aide. To her dismay, it was a confirmation that came from the other side. The Chinese NSA suggested, "Go for a ceasefire. Tell the Indians that both sides will get their military back to pre-war status."

She patiently listened and asked back, "Will they agree?" "They will, Indians are notoriously weak in diplomatic maneuvers." The call was hung up and she cleared her throat before having a glance at the black briefcase and continuing, "I am proposing an armistice to call an end to the conflict, both countries will get their armies to their pre-conflict positions."

A sudden proposal of peace from the country that was hell bent on a one sided victory would've aroused suspicion but because the world leaders saw the reason behind it, they quickly agreed fearing that further escalation might bring more devastation. However PM Verma outright refused. "What do you mean by that Prime Minister Verma, don't you want peace in the Asia Pacific?"

"Yes, I do want. But if China wants peace, it will be on our terms not on its. From our side, the conditions are pretty much the same. Both armies will move to their pre 1949 positions. Tibet will be a buffer nation between the two nations. All Chinese nuclear weapons will be destroyed under the surveillance of UN and Indian forces. People's Republic of China's membership in NSG and UNSC will be terminated permanently." He put forth his conditions, seriously annoying the Chinese President.

'What does he think? No, he knows that morale of our forces is low and is using it to his benefit. There's still hope, if we can lower the morale of Indian troops like they did ours, we can still hold on.' She thought, knowing that the fight was now not for expansion but survival. She looked at the briefcase that was already set for a second strike and pushed the 'FIRE' button without drawing any attention.

"What do you think you're about to do? You aren't in much of a strong position. Would you accept what India is asking?" President Ivan asked. President Rin gritted her teeth and replied, "No, I won't accept. We'll fight for our survival till the bitter end. I won't let those barbarian Indians take our civilized society."

Just as she completed, Ambassador Shreya rushed in the room with a call from the NSA. The phone was kept on speaker as the NSA spoke in rushed tone, "China has re-launched. Seven ballistic missiles from subs and three from inner mainland." "What?" PM Verma shrieked and looked at the Chinese President who gave a sinister smile.

"Prepare to intercept." He ordered and the NSA replied, "We're trying. As soon as we get a lock on the missiles..." PM Verma interrupted, "What are the targets?" "Delhi, Mumbai, Kolkata, Bangalore, Chennai, Vishakhapatnam and Hyderabad. We're yet to identify the targets of those from mainland."

PM Verma immediately retorted, "Use any and all resources to intercept them. As soon as it is done, hunt down those damn submarines in the IOR." He looked at the American satellite feed which now focused on the Indian sub-continent. Next moment, it picked up three bright flashes while the NSA added, "We have three confirmed nuclear detonations. Estimates are showing seven MT explosions at Chennai, Mumbai and Hyderabad. Airburst at 300 meters."

"What?" PM Verma was shocked as he tried to gauge the damages and casualty. "I know I shouldn't say this, but I really want to have you killed right now." She smirked and said, "Go on and try your luck. You still have four cities left." The comment left all leaders gritting their teeth in hatred. The NSA added, "Vishakhapatnam and Bangalore have been saved. INS Rajput has fired interceptors from its arsenal. We have confirmed airburst at 3000 meters; we have moderate blast damage to infrastructure in both cities."

"Good!!!" The entire meeting room sighed and PM Verma ordered, "Intercept all other missiles. Tell the CDS that he has the Level 1 Authority now. Immediately order evacuations in the nearby areas of the ground zero." The call wasn't hung and several minutes of silence passed. The screen changed from satellite feed to news.

Suddenly, a news headline caught everyone's attention. 'China calls an Emergency UNSC meeting to enforce a third party war-ending treaty between the two nations.' The entire room looked at the Chinese President who smiled as if teasing, 'Let's see whose demands are going to be fulfilled.'

The stares were broken by the Indian NSA who finally stated, "All missiles have been intercepted and destroyed by the space and air force. We have confirmed detonations but lost sixteen brave souls in the defense." "I'll take a report when I am back. Tell the CDS to hold the lines." PM Verma said before hanging the call and the Ambassador broke the phone.

PM Verma looked at the Chinese President with utmost hatred. "Well, it's true that Indians always play by rules. No matter how you play." She smirked and he thought, 'This meeting now has no meaning. If I play by the rules, I'll be the one who'd to accept defeat at Chinese terms.'

He sat on the chair and began to meddle with his briefcase. President John came to him and asked informally, "What are you doing? China's calling an end to this. Can't you guys just talk it over?"

PM Verma's face filled with rage as he yelled, "Talk it over? How ironic!!!" He rose looking straight into his eyes, "14 crore people were affected by this stupid endeavor and I don't even have an estimate on the environmental damages."

"So just have the Chinese pay for all that. You can go to the court for that..." He tried to stop PM Verma as he continued with the briefcase meddling. "I thought it was steadfast clear that this conflict was a local and non-nuclear one. This is the power of G-7...that hell of a nation just violated all norms of war in front of you and all you could do was just watch."

He took a breath and looked at everyone before continuing, "Anyone with even the presence of mind worth a dimwit will tell that this just a part of a well laid plan. China is seeing this as a victory and thinks that it can take anything it wants on the negotiating table and then I'll say that this is the last mistake they'll make."

President Rin smirked, "What an excellent speech, Mr. Prime Minister. I am pretty sure that next elections in India will be won by you. Though unfortunately, the table has been laid by us, if you back out all those years of propaganda that India is fighting a defensive war will be torn to shreds."

"Not very sharp as you claim to be." A smile emerged on PM Verma's face, "I didn't stop my forces for your silly rules. This is new India and I am okay as being seen as the aggressors. Because by the time I reach the negotiating table, there won't be any China to negotiate with."

Before anyone could react, he slid the briefcase towards Shreya. She caught the briefcase and asked, "Sir!!!" With a wicked smile, PM Verma said, "Ambassador Shreya, You're from Mumbai right." "Yes, I was but..." She replied without hesitation. "I am offering you a chance to take revenge, for you, for the 14 crore people who have been subjected to the horror and for all the 150 crore Indians."

"Wha~? Me?" She asked and he nodded, "Obliterate the country at will. No one will question your decision." Shreya looked around, her mind full of thoughts and dilemma, 'The Prime Minister has given me a chance of revenge. If they can kill us without hesitation, then ~' she cleared her mind of all hesitation and pushed the button.

The Ambassadors of all countries came in one by one with the intelligence chiefs on the phone line. President Ivan, who got the reports first, switched the LED to satellite feed again. The feed showed multiple launches from Indian submarines as they surfaced for short duration in South China Sea, Strait of Taiwan and the Philippine Sea.

"China can't intercept those ones. We took out their major missile facilities in the previous volleys, they're sure to hit." PM Verma commented. "What have you done Prime Minister? You should've at least thought about the future generations. You claim to be the oldest and most mature civilization, but you too..."

He interrupted the US president John, "A leader is a person who leads his country through everything. I don't want to be named yet another leader who lost everything that the soldiers won through their blood." UK's Prime Minister Bill asked half heartedly, "Can you at least tell us where they're going?" "Shanghai, Beijing, Tianjin, Shenzhen, Guangzhou, Chengdu, Chongqing, Dongguan, Shenyang and Wuhan. All are fifteen megaton." He replied and PM Bill turned towards Japanese PM Sugou, "They all launched from near your coast, can't you shoot them down."

"No!!!" PM Sugou replied, "In the first volley, both nations fired the missiles without provocation. So we intervened, but this is India's retaliation and if I help China to intercept them, it would be seen as an act of war by the Indians." President Rin yelled, "Then, why did you intercept our ones?" "I think I told you, this is retaliation. If India launched before you, I would've intervened but now it is India's right to do that."

PM Verma switched the LED to Israeli satellite feed that showed the destroyed cities due to the massive fireballs. The gigantic infrastructure centers which China was once proud of, and left untouched in the two year war was decimated. "The missiles were airburst. The fallout will clear within ten years." PM Verma said looking at the Chinese President who finally said, "We'll surrender."

17

Epilogue

May 14, 2040; almost four months after the Indian victory in the Battle in Gulf of Khambhat and all the nuclear chaos that followed, India was at peace. Redevelopment work began in most areas, except for the nuclear struck cities.

China surrendered on January 27, following a devastating nuclear exchange that left millions dead on both sides. UN sources claimed that despite extreme property loss in China, casualties in the exchange were roughly similar. On February 10, the two countries signed the ceasefire document in UNSC.

Under the surrender conditions, People's Republic of China was divided into three parts. The mainland China was now under joint control of US and Taiwan. Tibetan Autonomous Region was declared as an independent nation, though under military protection from India. All disputed lands were given to the other side. The Chinese colonies comprising of Pakistan, Sri Lanka, Myanmar and parts of Africa were monitored by UN as their regime underwent changes.

INHS Kalyani, Vishakhapatnam

It was almost a normal day in the Naval HQ of Vishakhapatnam. However in the medical wing, it was far more chaotic. It was the day when doctors decided to wake up 'The Miracle Girl' from her four month long slumber. She was rescued from the wreckage of the invincible ship that rocked the world on January 26 and has been recovering from her severe injuries.

In the ICU of INHS Kalyani, Ananya laid unconscious as the doctors removed the anesthesia and waited. About eleven in the morning, she slowly started to regain her consciousness but it took another two hours to get her completely aware. As soon as the doctors were done with her, a man in naval uniform entered the room.

He went to her side and shook hands with her. "So you're Ananya 'The Miracle Girl'? I am Warrant Officer Mehul Mishra, it's an honor to meet you." "What's this miracle girl thing about?" She asked bluntly. Mehul giggled and replied, "It's the name the entire navy has given you because of the miracles you did on the Chanakya. Moreover, the fact that you're alive after suffering so much is also a miracle."

Ananya stifled a giggle and replied, "Maybe, that's true." Mehul brought out a file and handed it over to her. "Please go through this." The file had 'CONFIDENTIAL' written on it and she opened the file with one hand to go through it page by page.

The door opened again and Amaira entered the room with Naina. Mehul immediately stood up and took his leave, leaving the file with Ananya who placed it on the side table. "It's nice to see you well captain." She said. Amaira looked at her, now completely different from the introverted and ferocious Ananya who was on the ship.

"Well, someone's awake after a long slumber." Amaira responded, smiling. The duo took a seat near her and began to talk. "Captain, actually I wanted to apologize for hitting you back then." Ananya began and Amaira gave an uncomfortable smile, "I'll get the accounts settled later on. But first, there's something everyone needs to know. What happened after everyone left? Why did you ram the ship into that carrier?"

Her cheerful face disappeared and was replaced by an uncomfortable look as she began, "It's a long story. Hope your superiors have enough time to hear all this." The statement left the duo in shock as she continued,

"After you guys left, I charged all available guns to ultra long range mode. My plan was to take out all the ships in a single salvo but it didn't work that well. Still in a couple of salvos it was done.

I figured that rescue would come soon, so I intended to wait till they came but...then I saw three people boarding the ship from the opposite side.

When I began to look around for them by the security cameras, I found out that armory personnel didn't leave.

I immediately used the internal communication apparatus to contact them and asked them to evacuate but they refused... Honestly, perhaps it was the toughest job to convince them to take the last lifeboat. However before leaving, the armory master ceded the feeder controls to the bridge.

I literally watched them to take the last lifeboat and leave me as the last one on the ship. Anyways, I quickly began to think on a way to get the ship out. I remembered that captain once said that the rudder module can be purged if the primary armor was purged as well.

So I checked the defense status, main hull was more-or-less intact but the armor was at two percent. That's when I purged the remaining armor along with the rudder module and started the propulsion system. The big idea was to get the ship in Indian Territory before the intruders could stop it.

But it got messed up when; they began to bang the door yelling surrender orders in English and Mandarin. I got no choice; I programmed the AI to ram the ship into the remaining carrier but not before emptying the entire armory. Almost the entire power was re-routed to just the propulsion, weaponry and the automated CIC. The acceleration was tremendous; before the intruders could enter we already reached 50 knots.

They blasted away the bridge's primary door with explosives – probably C4 or Semtex. There were three intruders; one was calling himself Admiral Wang and those two. That admiral was looking surprised initially on seeing me – but he gained composure when the boy whispered something in his ear.

He ordered me to take the ship to take the ship to the Chinese port of Gwadar. He repeated the order 'Take this battleship to Gwadar immediately.' By that time though, the ship was already on a collision course and the admiral noted the trajectory and decided to threaten me by his personal gun.

But till that time I had put the ship in complete manual lockdown. The ship began firing as soon as the probability index went beyond 0.2."

She stopped abruptly perspiring heavily. "What happened, you alright?" Naina asked, passing a glass of water. She drank the water and replied, "Yes, I am. Actually, I don't remember anything after that except getting shot twice maybe here and..." She involuntarily reached to her left chest about an inch higher than her heart but didn't pull her left hand.

Amaira stood up and went out of the room for a moment before returning. "Okay, everything that we speak now is off-records." She said as two more people followed her. Ananya knew one of them as Andrew, the American lieutenant commander whose team was rescued by the Chanakya.

The other guest was a little girl who was almost the same age as her. The little girl and Andrew walked up and took the seat on her left. "So, you're awake little miss." Andrew said with a smile. "Well, I am surprised that you're here. I thought you'd be in the US now."

He shrugged it off, "Well, I was. But I got special VISA to India. We are here to investigate the sinking of our fleet. Oh and meet her, she is my daughter Mary Gibbs." Mary gave a sweet smile and said, "Howdy. It's nice to meet you. Is everything pops told me about you true?"

Ananya gave an uncomfortable smile and replied, "I don't know what he told you." Everyone laughed and Ananya asked Amaira, "Where are lieutenant Vivaan and Arman?" "Oh, you aren't aware of that I guess. After all the diplomacy was concluded, Naina, Vivaan, Arman and I were promoted three ranks. Vivaan and Arman are in their respective ships. Naina and I are stationed here in Vishakhapatnam as in-charge for the rebuilding."

"Re-building?" She asked almost confused. Naina replied, "The day after the battle there was a high altitude nuclear interception here. Though casualty was zero, the damage to structural and power infrastructure was catastrophic. Because it is the naval headquarters, the responsibility of re-building of the entire city fell to our shoulders."

She walked to the window and removed the curtains. The view outside marveled Ananya, "I never expected to see the city in such a manner." Outside the window were multiple under-construction buildings and naval ships on the port. The building scheme was something entirely different than any other city.

"Well, it was decided to make this city into a complete naval stronghold. All buildings are being made to be self reliant and EMP resistant." Naina said as she closed the curtain and walked back. "Hey kid." Andrew whispered and Ananya bent towards him, "Did you tell anyone about our objective as you knew?"

"Not yet." "So, how about we get a deal?" Andrew whispered back. Ananya realized as she got three stares and sighed, "What deal?" "You won't tell anyone that we were monitoring your ship and in return I won't tell anyone that you sank my ship." Ananya gasped for air and asked almost audibly, "How'd you know?"

"Satellite imagery showed only your ship about 300 nautical miles away. And by what I have seen by my eyes, you can hit it. Don't worry; my higher-ups don't believe that anything other than a ballistic missile can travel that such a long distance." He smiled as Ananya sulked and nodded.

"So, what happened after the ship rammed with the carrier? And what happened to the trio?" Ananya asked. "Well, patrol teams were sent after the ship began to move abruptly. They knew that there was a crew member on board and two more rescue parties were sent as soon as the ships began to sink. The bridge had collapsed by then and they had to remove a lot of rubble to pull you out of it, barely alive." Naina said.

"As far as I've seen your reports, the orthopedic surgeon got his hands full. He had to replace more than six shattered bones." Amaira stifled a giggle as Ananya was creeped out. Looking quite interesting,

Mary got up and tried to look at her and found a faded elongated stitch mark on her right arm. "That's one."

She pulled the left hand which was jammed inside the blanket but Ananya resisted her attempt. "It's not funny trying to find replaced bones." Anyhow she pulled the blanket away in order to look at it, but what came out was surprising to all four of them.

Ananya's left arm was tethered to the bed frame by the means of a handcuff. Amaira, Naina and Andrew were bewildered, "What's the meaning of this?" Ananya responded, "I am held prisoner here. What's wrong about that?"

"Prisoner? On what account?" Naina asked and she passed the confidential file to her. "Your higher-ups somehow got their hands on my belongings and the infiltration stuff. I don't think that my tools were the things that got it messed." Amaira continued as Naina went through the file page-by-page, "The ID's would've."

"Yes, all my IDs were equally genuine. So, it created a doubt over my nationality. A court of inquiry was commissioned to scrutinize the IDs and they found that out." She paused as Naina finished the file and said, "This is totally crazy. She is charged with *'Striking senior officer'*, *'Disobedience'*, *'Espionage'*, *'Spying'*, *'Possessing top secret information as a foreigner'*, *'Falsifying data'* and *'Illegally participating in combat'*."

"What? In the US, all these charges are kinda guarantee that you'll get a death sentence." Andrew said and Amaira sighed, "She has four charges that attract death sentence, one life imprisonment and two seven year terms. I don't believe they'll do this." Her expression showed anguish over such a treatment to a teen.

"They have given me some time though, the court martial will begin one week after my rehab is completed and doctors declare me fit. If I prove that I am an Indian, all major charges will be dropped and rest will be pardoned. But..." Ananya said and Amaira asked, "But what, is there any problem."

"Yeah, kind of...they won't accept any document that I'll produce. Since all IDs are genuine, they believe that I have comrades in the governments as well." Ananya sighed at her helpless condition. Amaira wondered, "I don't understand how you are going to prove that you're an Indian." "I am blank." Ananya responded.

• • • •

AUGUST 20, 2040: ANANYA was declared fit and transferred to a military detention center. She was appointed a counsel to represent her in the general court martial. It was the first day of her court martial and a six member jury was appointed to judge her.

"Do you have any objections to the appointment of the jury panel?" The prosecution officer asked and she replied, "No." When everything was settled, the prosecution began its questioning.

"Miss Ananya Anand, were you the Weapons Control Officer aboard EXS-105, The INS Chanakya?"

"Yes."

"Do you know what crimes are you being tried for?"

"Yes."

"Well, I admire that you're not nervous. I hope you'll answer my next question as diligently."

"Go on."

"Why did you enlist?"

"It was a mandatory draft by the captain."

The prosecution went to his desk and pulled out a bag full of passports. He showed the passports to the jury and one of the members asked, "Are these passports yours?" Ananya looked at her counsel; when he met her the previous day in her cell he asked her to tell everything that's truth.

"This is not a normal court proceeding. If we manage to convince even a third of the jury that you've done nothing wrong, you might be spared of the death sentence." He said. Ananya nodded in affirmative, "Yes, all of them are mine."

"How did you get so many fake passports?" The jury asked. "Sorry to interrupt sir, but none of these hundred passports is fake. The investigation revealed that every passport is genuine and the background details are sound." The prosecutor interrupted.

Ananya looked at the defense counsel and sighed, "These are an important part of my profession." She looked at the prosecutor and said, "Before I volunteered in the navy." "Oh really, then would you mind telling this court what your profession was at such a young age?" The prosecutor asked.

"I..." Ananya began but paused to look at the defense counsel before continuing, "I was an infiltrator."

"So, do you admit that you're a spy?"

"No, I am not a spy."

"You just said that..."

"I am an infiltrator. That's different from a spy."

The jury asked, "How's it different from a spy?" Ananya turned towards the jury members and replied, "An infiltrator is nothing more than a soldier with tactical espionage skills." The prosecutor asked, "Oh really? Then why don't you showcase your so called 'tactical espionage skills.'"

Ananya sighed before saying, "Has your coffee arrived Lieutenant Deepak Kumar Das?" The simple statement left the entire court room surprised. The prosecutor stammered, "How do you know me?" "I even know that my original prosecutor has gone to Delhi owing to some urgent work."

The jury immediately took note and asked, "How'd you know all that?" "About the original prosecutor, I eavesdropped him talking to Commodore Milind Mehta outside the room. I know his name because I saw his ID in his wallet when he was paying someone." Lt.

Deepak was astonished by the observation and asked, "How'd you know about coffee?"

Ananya smiled innocently, "Before I entered the room, I saw someone leaving the room carrying a cup of tea. In this room here, we have a cup of tea along with a glass of water on every table except..." She pointed to the prosecutor's desk where only a glass of water was there. The jury discussed the matter and noted something.

Another jury member asked, "Even if we take into account that you're an infiltrator not a spy. The charges of espionage cannot be dropped even if spying is dropped. Which country are you affiliated with?" "I am Indian. So..." The prosecution interrupted, "And how can we believe that you're an Indian. Since you may not be knowledgeable but if you possess any other countries' citizenship, your Indian citizenship is revoked."

The jury added, "It is true and because you have so many genuine documents, your origin is in doubt." "We can let that one go aside for now. I will really be glad if you and your defense can prove you as an Indian. After all your actions aboard The Chanakya is well...beyond remarkable. But in that case, I'll like to have permission to interrogate then Commander and XO of the Chanakya, Ms Naina."

"Permission Granted." The presiding officer said and Naina went to the witness' podium. "Ms Naina, I want you to tell what happened when your captain gave the order to abandon ship and decided to stay back." Naina began, "All civilian officers left but we had an argument with the Captain..." The prosecutor interrupted, "Could you please skip to the main part?"

Naina looked at Ananya in the accused podium and said, "When we asked Weapons Officer Ananya to evacuate the bridge, she got up and slowly moved towards the exit. We were busy arguing and in the midst of that she knocked the captain unconscious." "Thanks. Ms Naina. Is that true Ms Ananya?" Lt. Deepak asked and she nodded in affirmative, "Yes, it's true."

The defense counsel stood up as the jury said, "Defense your witness, please!" "Ms Naina, as you know that she is being tried here for multiple crimes that she might not even know exist and you just testified against her. I wanted to ask what she hit the captain with to knock her out in one single hit."

"She hit her with her bare hands." He stopped her there and turned towards the jury. "As Ms Naina said, she hit the captain so hard by her hand to knock the captain unconscious in single hit. Sir, we all know that hitting someone hard to knock them unconscious is easy in movies and TV shows but in reality, it requires phenomenal strength. Something, I highly doubt that this teenager would possess."

The jury noted the point but the prosecutor asked, "But she just testified that..." "Let's ask her again?" "Ms Naina, let's be specific; what did you see exactly? No assumptions." Naina replied, "I was talking to the captain when she suddenly collapsed and Weapons Officer Ananya caught her from behind." The prosecutor said, "It was pretty obvious that she..."

"That's just an assumption." The defense counsel moved to his desk and pulled out some documents. "These are then captain Amaira's medical reports after she was brought on INS Himgiri." He passed the documents to jury and said, "It clearly says that she had a severe injury on her upper arm due to bullet wounds and was taking local anesthesia for pain management."

"Yeah, so what?" The jury asked. "I request permission to question our naval doctor, Dr. Raman to enlighten us on this." "Permission Granted." The doctor rose and switched places with Naina. "Dr. Raman, tell the jury why is local anesthesia given for pain control."

Dr. Raman began, "Sir, local anesthesia is a short term solution for pain management. It is mostly used when immediate pain relief measures are unavailable or the pain is insurmountable to be tackled by oral pain relief methods." "Can you give us a measure how much pain would the captain feel if the anesthesia begins to wear off?"

"Well...it's very difficult to give an estimate but if the anesthesia wears off, most of the patients pass out due to the pain." Dr. Raman said. "As the report say that the level of this pain killing anesthesia is very low. So what might've happened is when the weapons officer was leaving, the pain killing anesthesia wore off. This resulted in an intense pain signal getting to the brain and in order to cope up with it, the brain began to overwork. And as we know this leads to oxygen deficiency in brain and the person loses consciousness."

The reasoning seemed sound and almost acceptable. "Hmm...This is better than prosecution's reasoning." The presiding officer noted. "Ms Ananya, tell the court why did you want to be the last one on the ship. You were a civilian after all." Ananya thought for a while but couldn't answer. "Wasn't it because you knew some of your friends would arrive on the ship to get you and the ship."

The defense counsel reacted to the prosecution's statement, "What nonsense! Don't forget that her record as a crew member is almost spotless." The prosecutor retorted, "Then would you deny the fact that she was on the bridge with three Chinese sailors? Would you deny that the last conversation between them happened in Chinese? She maybe an infiltrator instead of spy, but her mission was to get the top secret information about the ship and hand it over to the Chinese."

Ananya stayed quiet, her face becoming more and more expressionless as the debate continued. The defense countered, "You should stop trying to harass her. We all have the translated version of the ship's log that housed this conversation. The captured Admiral of the Chinese fleet also testified that they didn't have any spies or infiltrators on board."

"Yeah, in that case would you like to tell us Miss Ananya, how you ended up in the same bunker as Captain Amaira on Camorta." The prosecution asked bringing out a worry some look on her face. The defense counsel reprimanded, "What do you mean by that? She went to the nearest one." "Then how come there were five Chinese spies in the same bunker as her and Captain Amaira."

Ananya slowly began, "I was there on an…" "Go on, why did you stop?" The prosecutor asked as she looked at the defense counsel and continued, "I was there on an assignment."

"And what was that? Scout the naval base?"

"No, I was on a lookout for Chinese spies in the base. I was on their tail for about three days before the attack."

"What a compelling story! But unfortunately, I don't think anyone here will believe it."

The defense counsel went to her and asked, "Why didn't you tell me this before?" Ananya stood still and replied after a long pause, "Like the prosecutor said, no one would believe this. So I left this part out." By 3:00 pm, the entire focus of the court martial shifted to her origins. Despite multiple claims about being an Indian, it seemed almost impossible to make the court believe so. Finally the court was adjourned with the jury instructing both the defense and the prosecution to prove her identity in one month.

Despite his best efforts, the defense counsel couldn't muster enough unbiased documents to prove that she was Indian. Though, the prosecution too failed in providing any reliable information. Embassies of all countries were contacted and though they do have the name in citizenship record, nothing else of any importance was found.

"All embassies have confirmed that they only have bare minimum information about her that is needed to get an official passport. On comparing to that, we have a lot of more paperwork available in India." The defense counsel noted but a jury member stated, "That's not enough for her to be declared an Indian."

The presiding officer and the jury members had some discussion and he said, "We have taken note of what both sides have to say about the matter. The jury shall proceed to give the verdict on October 7th 2040. The court is adjourned."

Days passed by painfully and finally on the day of verdict, there was a huge uproar. The media was allowed to report the verdict with only limited cameras inside the court. As everything settled down, the defense and the prosecution were allowed to make their closing statements.

"Even though her prowess in the decisive battle was remarkable, it doesn't mean that we can turn a blind eye to her blunders. It can never be overlooked that a person of non Indian origin had the controls of our most high-tech ship." The defense counsel continued after the prosecution, "Though her origins are in doubt, we cannot forget that she had risked her life multiple times to save the ship and its valuable crew. What we do now is going to set a landmark on how we treat war heroes."

The jury turned towards Ananya, who was wearing her naval uniform that she received upon her drafting. "Any closing statement from the accused?" Ananya who already had a depressed expression simply nodded in negative.

The presiding officer began, "This court shall now deliver the judgment. The jury has deemed Officer Ananya..." The entire court room waited in anxiety as the presiding officer continued, "...guilty of 'Espionage', 'Possessing top secret information as a foreigner', 'Falsifying data' and 'Illegally participating in combat'. With a majority of 4-2, the jury has sentenced Officer Ananya Anand to death."

The entire court was engulfed in clatters as the jury and Ananya as well left. She met Amaira and the naval crew outside the court room. They had an emotional exchange and when the guards came in to escort her away, Amaira said "Don't worry; we'll appeal in higher courts. It'll be all right." Ananya sighed and gave a weak smile before leaving.

In the next few months, Amaira and others filed appeal petitions in branch court and court of appeals. They tried their best to prove her nationality but didn't get any relief. Even though the prosecution's stand was weak as well, the benefit of doubt went to the prosecution instead of defense. After all military courts uphold the sentence; petitions were moved in the Supreme Court.

. . . .

JULY 12 2042, ALMOST two years have passed since Ananya's conviction by the court martial and her wait on death row. She was housed in Indian Navy's detention center isolated from other detainees. Only Amaira, Naina and others were allowed to meet her without any prior authorization.

In the evening of July 12, Amaira, Naina, Arman, Vivaan and Andrew visited her in the facility. They were led by the guards in the cell, where Ananya was reading a book. She bookmarked the reading page by folding the corner of the page and closed the book. Naina began, "Looks like you've got a new hobby."

Ananya who almost lost all of her cheerful nature over the years replied, "Yeah, I had to...I almost had a lot of free time with nothing to do. So, I requested the guards for this." They took seats in the not-so-large cell. Amaira began, "Tomorrow's the final hearing for the curative petition and..."

She paused to look at the teenager who for sure grew tired of the repeated court cases. Even though she was exempted by the Supreme Court from attending the court hearings physically and mostly attended them through video conference; the prolonged isolation and confinement did have its effects on her psyche.

"...The lawyer said that the case is finally on our side and most probably you'll be acquitted tomorrow." Amaira continued. "It'd be very nice." Ananya gave a weak smile as Arman reached out to the books she had. "Ramayana and Mahabharata, you sure got a strange taste. I thought kids never wanted to read such epics."

Ananya replied, "My father once said that the concept of infiltrators in India came out from these books. So, I wanted to read them once in my lifetime. Maybe after being released from here, I won't get a chance." After having a little chat in the cell, the group decided to leave.

As they fill the visitor's record, Naina noticed that another officer went in to visit her. As they snoop on the record, they read the reason 'OFFICIAL WORK'. Out of a whim, Amaira decided to stay back in order to have a talk to the officer. As he came out with an envelope in his pocket, Amaira caught him and pulled him to a corner.

"Who are you? I've seen your visitor entry too many times. And why do you always put the reason as 'OFFICIAL WORK'?" She asked and the officer tried his best to remember her. "I know you. You're Rear Admiral Amaira; you're the one fighting her appeals." He saluted hastily and she reiterated, "You didn't answer me."

"You know she was sentenced to death by the General Court Martial and upheld by all subsequent courts till now." "It's obvious, but it doesn't still answer my question." Amaira again asked. He began, "The court martial didn't tell how her sentence would be carried out. She earned the right to choose her death owing to her service in the war."

Amaira gulped, "Do you know what she chose?" The officer nodded in negative, "No, that's supposed to be a secret conversation between the convict and the executioner." "Isn't the right to choose death given only to those who have exceptional service records but are put to death for international war crimes?" Andrew emerged behind Amaira apparently eavesdropping everything.

Amaira replied, "Yes." "Then why don't they pardon her on that accord? You won the war, there's no-one who can question your decisions over this matter." The officer replied to Andrew's question, "I know how you feel. She's supposed to be a war hero but tomorrow she'll die. I too feel sorry for her but we can't go against the rules."

"What? Tomorrow?" Amaira asked in shock and wanted to go in to confront Ananya but the officer stopped her. "No, you can't disturb her now. You should wait for at least half an hour." Andrew asked,

"Why so?" "She is...right now, she is writing her will. The warden will tell me when she's done. Actually, I am a bit surprised that she didn't tell you. But unless the Supreme Court puts a stay on her execution, she will be executed on July 13, 2042 at exactly 12 noon."

The warden came out after twenty minutes and gave the file to the officer who took his leave. By the time, Amaira had called the entire group and explained the situation to them. Most of them were surprised by the information and Naina noted, "The hearing starts at 11 in the morning. It means they'll have only an hour to win the case. I highly doubt the court will put a stay on this."

Amaira nodded in agreement as they walked inside the detention facility to meet Ananya again. The curative petition was a last ditch effort to prove her nationality. As they entered her cell, Amaira asked directly "Why didn't you tell us that your sentence is to be carried out tomorrow?"

Ananya was curled up in a corner, probably trying to sleep. "I didn't want to burden you with this. Actually, I never wanted you to bother filing my appeals and curatives. You were just delaying the inevitable." Naina asked surprisingly, "Why? Don't you want to live?"

Ananya rose to her feet and said, "What would I do? Living here continuously for one year nine months and five days, with only exposure to the outside world during the court hearings, even death would be better than this." Tears began to flow from her eyes as she broke down, crying.

For the first time since they met, the naval officers realized that she was still a teen. They let her cry, letting her vent out the disappointment and frustration that she built up over time. As she gained control, Amaira tried to console her as she continued, "You know, I was trained during the Indo Chinese Cold War period. My missions came during the war and here after the war, I don't even have an identity. I couldn't even prove that I am an Indian and no country would accept me because my own country didn't..."

"But that's not a reason to give up on life. You're so brave..." Andrew said but Ananya interrupted, "It's not true. I am a total coward; I couldn't even bring myself to end this suffering. Captain...I mean Rear Admiral; there is something I want you to know before I die. I wasn't the last one on the ship for letting everyone escape...I was there...because I knew that this'll happen and I wanted to be instead listed as KIA." Amaira clenched her fist and exercised the utmost control to not get violent with her. "What if tomorrow you're acquitted before the execution?"

Ananya wiped her tears and said, "I'll find a new purpose to live. I'll forget about everything that happened between these walls and start anew." Amaira immediately left the cell and went stomping out. Outside the facility, she vented out her frustration on the lush green grass.

"Your contact does have the homework right. If you want, I can have her transported out of India and no one would ever find out what happened." Andrew suggested but Amaira brushed him off, "There's no need. I know they'll win tomorrow, but the time is of essence." She dialed a number and talked with the person for few minutes before hanging up.

"That's easier said than done." Vivaan said. Naina agreed, "Yeah, we always took her and her mental fortitude for granted. I don't think she could ever come out of this." Amaira initially mistook Vivaan's statement but realized the premise when Arman added, "The trauma she faced right from Camorta upto now is overwhelming even for battle hardened personnel. It'll be another miracle if she ever comes out of it." Amaira however, remained positive "Don't be so pessimistic. You know she is called 'The Miracle Girl', she can make out of it."

· · · ·

JULY 13 2042: ANANYA was set to be executed on the military drill ground of Vishakhapatnam by firing squad. The execution was not covered by media but on Ananya's special request, all her friends from the Chanakya were allowed to witness the event. The drill ground had about a hundred spectators including Amaira, Naina, Vivaan, Arman, Divya, Andrew and the Americans.

At 11:45, Ananya was brought out into the ground escorted by four men. She wore a white T-shirt over black legging and a grey knee length skirt. In the middle of the ground was a pole to which she was tied. After ensuring immobility, the field officer offers her a blindfold which she refused politely, "I've already died a lot of times. Like every time, I face death head on."

The field officer smiled gently and whispered in her ear, "I am really sorry for this. Please forgive me in the name of your God." Ananya smiled and nodded. The field officer retreated backward and sighed, "Tomorrows headline in the news will be 'Execution of a 17 yr old war hero by firing squad.'"

He blew the whistle and eight men came with automatic rifles. Standing between the men and Ananya was a black curtain over a cardboard wall. The field officer waited for the clock to hit 11:55 and ordered, "Train your guns!" The men loaded the magazines into the rifles and stepped forward.

Time ticked away slowly as the field officer yelled another order, "Prepare to fire." The eight men removed the safeties as the clock hit 11:58, the triggers creaked under gradual pressure. "It's going to be over soon." Ananya muttered to herself and smiled. She turned her head towards the crowd on her right and let out a deep breath.

Time slowed down as Amaira looked away from the field with a jerk. "I can't believe they couldn't even buy time from the court." "It's time that you face the truth. Its less than a minute now but she'll be remembered in military history forever..." Naina paused to look at another officer rushing in with a file and envelope.

"Look over there." Someone in the crowd shouted and everyone's gaze shifted to the field officer who opened the envelope and read it. After going through the letter, he shouted "Hold your fire." He then opened the file and after minutes of reading and conversing with the other officer, he said "Lower your rifles men. The execution is cancelled."

The eight men did as they're ordered. They re-engaged the safeties and lowered the rifles. The field officer removed the curtain and went to a surprised Ananya. "What happened?" She asked as he undid the binds and he replied almost whisperingly, "The Supreme Court declared you an Indian. All the charges are dropped. Congratulations, you're free." A wave of cheer ran among the crowd as she was taken out of the drill ground.

As she came out from the detention center with her belongings, finally as a free and guilt-free person after an hour; she found the entire crew of the Chanakya waiting for her. The entire crew thanked her for the heroic battle two years ago as they never got a chance to meet her since then.

"You've grown so much..." Divya said. The four naval officers and the Americans looked from a distance as she meddled with the crowd. She looked much different than the depressed and gloomy Ananya on the death row. After sometime, she approached Amaira and smiled, "I must admit Rear Admiral; you kept your end of bargain."

Joe looked at her, remembering the day when she toyed with him aboard the Chanakya. "She looks so different, is she still that strong?" He asked the next sailor who replied, "Why don't you check that in a brawl?" Ananya seemed to hear the conversation, "As much as I'd love to have a fight with you, but fighting here could brew trouble for us."

"Nah...She's not the same..." Joe replied but Ananya quickly grabbed one of his arms and twisted it completely before abruptly leaving it. She whispered in his ear while comforting her arms, "I just don't want to go behind bars again, given that I just came out after two years." The group laughed but noted that her ferocity did wear out after two years of solitary confinement.

Amaira smiled, "Well, honestly I am still mad over yesterday's conversation. But anyways, I kept my end of bargain and I hope you'll keep yours. But right now, you have a hectic schedule for at least a month." Amaira gave her a small mobile which unlocked upon being touched on the screen.

A memo presented itself on the screen and her eyes bulged out, but kept herself from exclaiming. "Well, you had every reason to be mad at me. But isn't this too much." Amaira smiled and pointed to a car waiting behind her, "Oh, your schedule starts as soon as your final belongings are brought out."

"Final belongings~?" Ananya wondered as the warden came out with a file and some gift wraps. He gave the items to Ananya as she recognized the items, "My will!" Naina asked, "What'll you do with them?" Ananya smiled and handed them to Amaira, "I'll give them to the intended person anyway."

Amaira opened the gift wraps which were packed with a lot of time, to reveal three books. Two of them were the epics she had, though with a lot of bookmarks and third one a hand-written diary. Amaira looked at Ananya who smiled, "I felt it like a responsibility to pass on my skills and knowledge. So over two years, I wrote down every single technique and skill I knew."

"But why me?" Amaira asked as they moved towards the car. "I told you back on the ship that you could be a better infiltrator. So, that's why I chose you as my successor." "You make it feel like it's some sort of a hereditary title." Amaira paused as she asked the driver to get them to the airport.

Upon arriving at the airport, Amaira immediately took the boarding pass to the next flight to Delhi. Though Ananya wanted to change the set of clothes, Amaira didn't allow that as they were short on time. Since they took the special military entrance, there wasn't much of a crowd. They had minimal interactions with the people in the waiting area and boarded the flight.

"Things won't be that easy in Delhi. Almost whole India knows that you're coming to Delhi." Amaira whispered in her ear. "I'll manage to sneak out if they don't that know I am coming with you." She giggled and said, "That won't be needed. I was just informing you."

The flight landed in Delhi, about two hours after take-off. They went out of the airport easily and headed straight towards the Joint Military Wing. "I am surprised Captain...I mean Rear Admiral, I thought we would be stuck in a crowd." Amaira smiled and explained, "We didn't go to the normal civilian terminals like others. The security sent us through the military terminal."

Ananya relaxed a bit and sighed, "That saved a lot of trouble. The system has changed a lot since I last came here." "You didn't appear in any Supreme Court hearing did you?" Ananya looked outside the armored car as they rode through the capital.

As the car stopped outside the Joint Military Wing's building in New Delhi's reconstructed Central Vista, she saw the massive media buildup there. "What's going on?" Ananya asked nervously and Amaira said with a gentle smile, "Don't be nervous. Just try to be as calm as you can be and don't interact with them no matter what. Okay!" Ananya nodded and both of them came out of the car and went inside through the media buildup.

"Hurry, we're behind schedule." Amaira said as they went past the security checks. The duo rushed in the complex as Amaira led the way and Ananya caught upto her. The duo stood in front of a double door when Ananya finally asked her, "What's happening? At least tell me what the big idea is."

Amaira knelt to a knee as she mended Ananya's dress and said, "The navy has decided to declassify all Chanakya's documents. And what better way to do this than by a master of propaganda." Ananya gave a suspicious look and nodded in agreement. "Be a little cheerful, you're a war hero – a celebrity."

The doors opened and the duo entered the room filled with media personnel. On the center table was, Subhash Mukherjee – CDS of Indian Armed Forces, Field Marshal Yash Kumar – Chief of Indian Army, Admiral of Fleet Simarjeet Singh – Chief of Naval Staff, Marshal of Air Force Tarun Chandrashekhar – Chief of Indian Air Force, Specialist Narendra Tiwari – Chief of Indian Cyber Force, Space Marshal Shivaji Srivastava – Chief of Indian Space Force and General Samuel Bhabaji Trivedi – Chief of Indian Missile Forces.

Along with them was Admiral Abhijeet of Indian Navy's Eastern Fleet. All media personnel turned back to greet the two ladies. The two of them went to the stage where two seats were empty with their names written over a plate. The press conference began as Amaira and Ananya took their seats.

CDS Mukherjee began, "Gentlemen, as you know that we are declassifying all the documents of INS Chanakya and its decisive voyage. So, we would like to have Rear Admiral Amaira and Miss Ananya to do the honor." Amaira and Ananya took the file from Fleet Admiral Simarjeet and removed the knot to reveal the documents.

A copy of documents were provided to the media and after sometime a reporter asked, "Is it true that it was the Navy that filed and fought the appeal and curative petitions of Miss Ananya?" Fleet Admiral replied, "Yes, in fact Admiral Abhijeet and Rear Admiral Amaira represented and collected the evidence."

Another one asked, "Admiral Abhijeet, how'd you manage to prove that she's an Indian in the Supreme Court? All other courts have given the benefit of doubt to the prosecution." Abhijeet began, "We had all records of Sadashiv Anand, crew member of Seafarer – the ship that was sunk in the Malacca disaster. He is Miss Ananya's biological brother and since the prosecution couldn't provide any records of her giving up her Indian citizenship, she was acquitted today on the basis of benefit of doubt."

"Miss Ananya, is it true that you were moments away from being executed when your release order came?" Another one asked and Ananya responded, "Yes, it is true." Another reporter asked putting his arm in the pocket, "Miss Ananya, the nation wants to know why you volunteered to be the last one standing on that decisive battle instead of letting the experienced officers do that?"

The question froze Ananya for a moment and she didn't answer it. The same question was asked in the court martial multiple times and never went down good. Amaira asked the reporter to exercise control over the questions. The reporter changed the question, "Rear Admiral Amaira, then would you explain how the Chinese managed to tail your ship throughout the entire journey from Camorta to Gujarat."

Amaira replied, "The ship wasn't designed with stealth capabilities. We only had to rely on enemy's technical shortcomings for short term stealth." Another reporter stood up, "Miss Ananya, your Intel reports on Chinese vessels and bases are also public. How did you get these?"

Ananya looked at Amaira who had given her the official stance of the navy through the phone. 'You are a first generation infiltrator and take up missions and skills on your own discretion. No one taught you this.' She let out a deep breath and said, "I have been scouting Chinese vessels and bases as an infiltrator way before the war began."

"How much time has it been?" Another reporter asked. Ananya thought for a while and replied, "Seven years; give or take..." The audience gasped as they comprehended the fact that she did this since she was ten years in age. A foreign reporter asked, "Doesn't the Indian Armed Forces owe an apology for all the trouble and trauma she had to suffer."

Before any of the chiefs could say anything, Ananya interrupted, "No, they don't owe any apology of sorts. I was prepared for this, the moment I decided to begin infiltrating the enemy bases." Another reporter asked, "Even for the death by firing squad as you were sentenced?" Without any hesitation and re-thinking she added, "Yes! I had nothing to fear, I've died a lot of times to fear death in first place."

"So, what will happen to her now that the war is over and she is known far and wide?" Another reporter asked. This time CDS said, "Owing to the new kind of warfare she indulged in, the Chiefs of all Indian Armed Forces have unanimously decided to learn this new form of warfare and make best possible use of it."

The six chiefs nodded as the CDS continued, "Thereby, Miss Ananya's education will be continued from when it was discontinued and after evaluating her expertise in various fields she'll be allowed to teach interested officers in her field. Her expertise with the experimental Chanakya ship will also help us fine-tune the next generation Chanakya Class Long Range Assault Ships."

· · · ·

ON JANUARY 26, 2043: Exactly three years after fateful and decisive battle in the Second Sino-India War, Ananya was awarded Paramveer Chakra by the President of India. The Navy retained her under their command till her education and official training ended in 2045.

---

[1] Siliguri Corridor is a 10 km stretch in West Bengal crucial for joining North Eastern states with Indian mainland

[2] POW: Prisoner of War

[3] CIC : Combat Information Center

[4] XO : eXecutive Officer

[5] CIWS : Close In Weapon System

About the Author

Ayushya Verma is a Kid from the new India that sees that the national security of a country is more important than anything.